THE DARK SCAR

Oroni Tendera

Worlds Unknown Publishers

Worlds Unknown Publishers
2515 E Thomas Rd,
Ste 16 -1061
Phoenix, AZ 85016-7946

www.wupubs.com

For my parents Mark Meshack Oroni
and Stella Nasaba Mwembula.

C H A P T E R

1

"Campus isn't a convent," said Nuru as he walked to the balcony of his room on the sixth floor of Kilimanjaro Hostel. Earlier that morning, he had attempted to write a poem, only to stare at a blank blinking laptop screen for forty minutes. He fought writer's block by feeding his eyes on campus denizens. Even though it was a Thursday morning, Taifa University roared with life, laughter, love and violence. Every day was like a wild weekend.

Students thronged everywhere: Christian Union students clutching Bibles under their armpits, whiskey connoisseurs staggering out of Zawadi Pub, love birds walking in pairs to various hostels and loud students sitting outside Miriam Makeba Multipurpose Hall waiting for their lecturer.

Nuru shifted his gaze to the azure sky—partially covered by clouds ranging from immaculate white to dark grey. To the east, the sun glowed like an orange ball. Wind blew across the atmosphere, forcing scattered clouds to move towards each other, forming a gigantic fluffy cloud whose size continued to increase slowly. Conscious of time, Nuru took in a deep breath and walked back to his room.

On his desk, the blank page on his laptop screen was still waiting for him to fill it with words. It haunted him. Nuru pushed the laptop aside and took a pen and paper. He abandoned the idea of writing a poem. He was going to write a romance novel. He tried to resuscitate his creative writing energy by shaking his head, but the image of his girlfriend, Amani, materialized in his mind, blocking him from exploring that literary genre. He stopped thinking about the structure of his prospective literary project and started writing:

"It's 9:00 a.m. The adjacent laptop casts its harsh light, glaring at my paper, pen and I. A bone-soothing breeze is blowing into my room, thanks to the open door. For that reason, my thin hairy legs are partially parted. My back is arched forward; face elongated.

I've been waiting for inspiration to strike for the past hour. "What am I supposed to write?" I wonder. "Write anything literary. You'll 'literally' start from there," I muse. My fingers clasp around my pen. I hold the pen tightly above the paper, trembling. "I shall write an absurd drama. Like the theatre of the absurd, life is a repetition of empty clichés and mysteries. No, life is no mystery. I shall write a tragedy. Like a tragedy, life is a journey whose final destiny is darkness. No, writing a tragedy is a heroic but horrific experience. I have to write a high comedy No, our society is too lazy to unearth humour in a high comedy. What of penning a poem? A sonnet that blends Shakespearean and Italian structures. No, that sounds too scholarly.

I tilt my pen. My head snaps with a click. I feel a sharp pain crawl down my spine. My pen jumps out of my hand. I slump deeper into my seat. "I want to write right now," I cry.

The whole of my body is immobile. My neck is stiff. My eyes are pulsating with pain. My lower and upper teeth have become inseparable. My hanging lips have grabbed each other. I can't stick out my long tongue. I can't think. I can't see. I can't feel. I can't smell. Am I slipping into a comma?

My alarm shrills. "I must write before it is too late," I mutter. I struggle to lift my head, but it falls back to the headrest. I manage to lift my right hand, albeit painfully. I get hold of the pen. My hands are shaking. My head is still on the headrest. "I shall write my own writing," I groan. My pen slides on paper. Little by little, a letter is written. Words are woven, a sentence is structured, and a paragraph is crafted. I don't know how this writing will end—what climax it will come to. I'm just writing. Writing because I have something to write that I must write. Therefore, I am writing. By the way, I'm not writing a play, poem, short story, piece of flash fiction, novel, or novella. This is my own writing, flowing freely from my heart, head, hand, and finally falling on paper. As I write, my right hand becomes light. My head is jerked from the headrest to an upright position. My biceps contract and relax involuntarily. I feel fresh warm air fill my lungs. Renewed energy entangles my body. I write, write, and write. Will I write forever? As I write, I read what I'm writing. As I read what I'm writing, I see my fears on paper. I shudder. As I read what I'm writing, I smell my fungi-infected foot; I laugh at my ignorance. As I read what I'm writing, I perceive my pride as well as shame. I fidget. Nonetheless, my pen dances nonstop to the rhythm of write-read. My eyes, running through my writing, are seeing slanting characters. My ears are listening to the sound of my pen waltzing on paper. My sweaty vibrating nose smells fresh ink on paper. The tip of my thumb, index finger, and middle finger, feel the hard pen as the honed edge of my palm caresses the crispy paper. My pen stops spitting ink. "What the hell!" I curse. It's running out of ink. "Where is another pen? I shall write to my grave," I scream. "Where is another pen? I shall write to my grave," I hear the echo of my voice immortalized on paper."

Writing had carried all his sensibilities. Nuru was so engrossed in it that he was unable to honour his phone alarm, reminding him of an impending morning lecture. He checked his phone. There were three missed calls from Amani. He dialed her phone number, but his call was ended with a text message: *"Hi, where are you? You're forty minutes late for the lecture."*

Turning up late for a lecture did not trouble him as much as failing to write when he felt the need to do so. He locked his room and walked downstairs to Garang Lecture Hall without any hurry or worry. The lecture hall was full to capacity. Professor Mubiru was giving a PowerPoint presentation. Amani occupied a back seat. Beside her was an empty seat reserved for him. He patted her gently on the back before sitting. Startled, she shrieked, attracting the attention of the whole lecture hall. At his sight, she smiled. He grinned.

"Pay attention. We were talking about the goals of education. The second goal is education for national unity. As a matter of fact, we are from different cultural, ethnic, economic, religious, and geographical backgrounds converging here with one primary objective: to be educated. As you go about the process of acquiring relevant skills, instructors should impart on you appropriate attitudes that will enable you to appreciate each other despite your differences. Remember, we are many but one people. You need me, and I need you. That is the way to national cohesion.

"The third goal of education is education for international consciousness. Education should make students appreciate the culture of other people in various parts of the world. It should enlighten you about the ways of the South Sudanese, Indians, Mexicans, and Australians."

"Was the lecturer reading his past?" wondered Nuru.

Sensing his uneasiness, Amani drew her seat closer to him and looked directly into his eyes. He could not help but recollect how she had entered his life.

"Comrades, power!" shouted Angela.

"Power!" The audience responded.

"You are very dull. This is the Literature Students Association. An organization for poets, playwrights, novelists, thespians, and lovers of literature. All freshmen are welcome. Before you introduce yourselves, I would like to engage you in a session of teasing. Just for the sake of breaking the ice. I'm starting with that dude sitting over there," said Angela while pointing a finger at Nuru.

"This guy has such a big head that his dreams come in series," said Angela making the audience to burst into laughter.

"Angela, your father is so greedy that he swallowed his own Adam's apple," Nuru hit back.

"Angela has excessive Hazundaism to the extent that when she's sent money via mobile money, she examines the message against the sun's rays to assess the authenticity of the money," belted out a back bencher in an exaggerated soprano voice. Unlike the other teases, the latter drove the whole hall into thunderous laughter for about two minutes.

"The last tease by that lady was the funniest, but it's very stereotypical in nature," pointed out Angela.

"Nooo!" The audience roared in disapproval.

"Excuse me. It's impolite to generalize certain traits found among a few members of a particular ethnic group. Not everybody from Hazunda tribe is filled with avarice. I call that argument a fallacy of sweeping generalization. Remember what organization this is. As lovers of literature, our main mandate is to educate, enlighten, and dismantle stereotypes in our society."

"Madam Chairperson, please stop giving us long boring lectures. We need to work on today's main agenda: welcoming first year students and open mic poetry," interrupted a young man.

"Yes," the audience chorused to approve him.

"Fine. All freshmen please stand and give us your first name and any other detail that you feel is relevant."

Nuru was standing adjacent to Angela. Therefore, he was the first student to introduce himself.

"My name is Nuru Ntendo. I love poetry and music. What else would you like to know about me?"

"Your marital status," a husky voice demanded.

"Single and searching."

The last person to introduce herself was Amani. She stood up, cleared her throat and said, "My name is Amani. I'm double majoring in Linguistics and Literature. I have an indescribable passion for literature and politics. Concerning my marital status, I'm single and satisfied."

Her last statement elicited murmurs. Nuru turned to get a better view of her. She was slender and dark skinned. Her hair was short and curly. Nuru almost got hypnotized by her beauty but struggled to look composed.

"Order please. Let's move to our second agenda: open mic poetry. If you've got a poem that you'd like to share with us, please feel free to come on stage and perform it. Foreigners have always described Nchi as a country of poverty and poetry—a dancing, dying nation. I call Nchi a country of poetry and tribal stereotypes. Ladies and gentlemen, the floor is yours."

The first poet performed a poem entitled "Sour Love," which did not ignite much reaction from the audience. Amani was the fifth poetess, and her poem, "Confessions of a Caged Feminist," frenzied the audience but this was nothing compared to Nuru's poem, "Identity I Need to Know."

Nuru had mastered the art of capturing the attention of his audience. He ran to the stage, studied the audience for four seconds then begun to sing the unofficial national anthem of Nchi composed by a celebrated Nchian musician. The song called for unity. After realizing that the audience was completely submerged in the song, he said, "Ladies and gentlemen, open the doors to your emotions for "Identity I Need to Know . . .

Am I black, tall, short, thick, slim?
You say I look like a Buba
But do I care?
You say I'm boastful
So, my tribe must be Mbayuyu
You say I consume a lot of food
So, I am a Tetung

I love money
So, I must be a Hazunda
My son slapped your son
And you branded me a Jaiti there and then
Who am I?
I need to know my identity.

You say I'm an immigrant
Just because my accent sounds Rwandese?
You say my great grandfather was South Sudanese
Just because I'm tall dark and handsome?
You think one of my parents is Nigerian
Just because my brother duped you and took all your cash?
Who am I?
I need to know my identity.

Why are you branding me names?
The poverty-stricken
The second citizen
The war-torn
The sleeping giant
The beggar
The overgrown child
Who am I?
I need to know my identity!
Thank you."

Cheers, claps, and whistles followed Nuru's performance. "Indeed, that was a brilliant performance from Nuru Ntendo," remarked Angela.

"I beg to differ. That string should not be called a poem. It lacks unity and sounds like random lines forcibly stuck together," said Daniel.

"Who else thinks Nuru's poem doesn't deserve to be the best?"

Silence ruled.

"So, 'Identity I Need to Know' is the poem of the day?"

"Yes," The audience agreed.

"Since we're running short of time, we won't have a comprehensive poetry criticism session. I declare the meeting adjourned."

As everyone dispersed, Nuru stood at the door, holding his breath and waiting for the lady who had driven him crazy at first sight.

She was as tall as he, and walked elegantly like an international fashion model on a runway. As the distance between the two melted, he leaned against the door

"Hi Amani," said Nuru while scratching his clean-shaven head to display his massive biceps.

"Hi. Nuru, the poet laureate. How are you? Your poem was a masterpiece."

"I'm humbled. Getting such a comment from a combination of beauty and brains is no mean feat. Thank heavens I'm the lucky one today," said Nuru as he patted his wide chest.

They exchanged phone numbers and social media usernames amid jokes and laughter. Nuru didn't fail to use his gift with words. During the first two months, Amani used to dismiss him incessantly with a flat stereotypic statement:

"Men from Buba tribe are serial heartbreakers." But a semester later, the two were like conjoined twins.

"What's the problem, Nuru? You look lost in thought?" whispered Amani while poking his head.

"Just a little flu. It's troubling me," he replied amid feigned coughs.

"Get well soon, dear."

"Thank you."

"Remember I'm still the beauty with brains. You're either kidding or concealing something from me. Aren't you?"

Nuru shook his head sideways.

"Let me guess. This lecture has made you recall how I became part of you? The way I used to despise men from your ethnic group?"

"That's history. Let's concentrate on the lecture lest we score Es on our end-of-semester examinations."

"Murmurs from the back benchers are interrupting us. We are dealing with a very important subtopic: national goals of education."

As the lecturer concluded his statement, a dozen young men dressed in black suits and dark sunglasses stomped into the lecture hall.

"Those are members of Corporal Squad," said Nuru.

"What the hell is Corporal Squad?" A student sitting in front of Amani inquired.

"Cartels of Taifa University," replied Nuru.

They formed a semi-circle around the lecturer. One of them—stocky and bald, weighed down by a bushy walrus moustache—moved to the lecturer. He snatched the microphone from him and screamed, "Comrades power!"

"Power!" a few students in the hall responded.

"No, this is my class, and you have no right to arrogantly interrupt it," cried the lecturer as he attempted to repossess the microphone.

"We are here on an important mission. We are here to fight for the rights of comrades. We can't sit back and watch in silence as the administration makes fools out of us. Why should the administration postpone yet again the students' union elections till the next academic year?"

"That's not fair," a voice cried.

"This is another plot by the vice chancellor to bring in a candidate from his Jaiti tribe. All that Jaiti people know is how to cheat in elections," a young man shouted.

"To solve this problem, my fellow comrades, we're going to lead a peaceful demonstration to the vice chancellor's office and order him to respect our rights. Comrades power!"

"Power!" The response was deafening.

"We go. We go," students chanted as they marched out of the lecture hall.

Even though the demonstration was termed peaceful, anything that appeared in their sight was destroyed completely. Flower beds were turned into playing grounds, eucalyptus trees growing along the pavements were cleared, and window panes were smashed. The students' centre was not spared either. It was broken into, and hundreds of litres of wine, spirits, and beer were looted.

Police sirens rang through the air as dozens of tear gas canisters were pelted at the rowdy students. Empowered by arrogance, a bunch of students ducked the tear gas canisters and hurled them back to the officers. Taifa University became so chaotic that students were ordered to vacate the campus within an hour.

CHAPTER 2

The sun sent its golden rays to the ground, forcing water vapour to rise. Beside a drying bush that once had been a vigorous labyrinth, a black mamba slithered out of its burrow and coiled its jet-black body around a twig to enjoy the pleasant morning sun. Birds, too, were fascinated by the sun. They chattered and chirped, swooping and flying freely in the miasma.

Across the valley, on the rolling plains of Lakira, a flock of sheep appeared unmoved by the serenity of the morning sun. They concentrated on their own business: chewing grass. Nuru enjoyed the picturesque view of Lakira village from the top of Lakira hill, centrally located in the village.

A strong whirlwind blew past him, without warning, leaving grains of soil in his eyes. Nuru rubbed his eyes until tears welled up in them. He clicked and continued to bask as he enjoyed the glamorous scene of his home village. Little did he know that another disappointment was imminent. The sun was swathed in dark grey clouds.

"Nothing shall stop the sun from shining. Nothing shall kill the sun; not even the midnight darkness. After all, hasn't it attempted countless times? And still, the sun has not been slain. It has continued to emerge every morning, full of zeal and youthful energy," mused Nuru.

He recalled his elementary science lesson. Sunlight and water are essential components for photosynthesis to take place- the process by which green plants produce food that sustains the planet earth. Therefore, the world would starve to death in the absence of either water or the sun.

Nuru's face brightened up with a smile at this thought. The dark clouds turned into Amani's image. The sun was left exposed, shining. After a few seconds, Nuru saw his reflection in the sun. It wasn't really his reflection; he was the sun, shining bright and brighter while Amani was the nimbus cloud, growing fat and fatter.

"No, this is weird. This is very weird. It can't be true," Nuru screamed.

"Wake up. It is already 11:00 a.m. and you're still in bed," Mrs. Ntendo yelled at her son.

"This is absolutely absurd," he continued screaming.

"What is the problem, my son? Have you been bewitched?"

"I'm sorry, mama. It was just a dream."

"I knew that woman was after something."

"What's the name of the woman you are talking about?" Asked Nuru as he rose from his bed

"My son, you don't need to be a magician to see."

"Mum, come on. Get to the point. What is it?" Pleaded Nuru while assuming an upright sitting posture on his bed.

"Aren't you aware that Mr. Gapedo, our neighbour, sold a portion of his land to a couple from Gebo land? As a matter of fact, the Gebo people are notorious for witchcraft and spiritualism."

"Mum, stop jumping to accusations."

"My son, I wish you were old enough; you would comprehend what I'm talking about. That couple has been picking quarrels with your father over our land boundary. They're so stubborn and keep on extending the boundary into our farm every night. Thank God your father is more than a tiger. He's been fighting back without tiring. Since that couple's evil plans have failed countless times, who knows what they're plotting?"

"So, mum, you're suggesting that by the virtue of our new neighbours being from the Gebo tribe, they're automatically sorcerers?"

"In fact, calling them sorcerers is an understatement. From the time those devils set their feet on our land, epidemics and calamities have never ceased to strike. Yesterday, your university was closed indefinitely because of a violent students' protest. Now, demons have been cast on you. May the Lord save us," Mrs. Ntendo screamed as she walked out of her son's room.

Nuru discovered that the dark scar on his mother's neck had developed white lesions.

"Mum, by the way you have never told me what caused such a terrible scar on your neck. It keeps on staring at me with a deeper horror each time I look at it."

Mrs. Salo stood still suddenly. Her face contorted. Tears welled up in her eyes making them to look glassy. She blew her nose, then swallowed a huge lump of saliva before opening her mouth.

"The gaping wound in my heart is yet to heal. Pus is still flowing out of my hurt heart. My son, it is a sad story. I think you are old and strong enough to comprehend this tragedy that I'm about to narrate. A true story of a neighbour turning against a neighbour. A true story of a human being deeming a fellow human an outcast. It's madness, my son. "

Mrs. Ntendo composed herself and narrated to her son the story behind the dark scar on her neck. At some point, she broke down in tears as she spoke.

Twenty years ago, when the Ntendos were watching the 7pm news in their magnanimous living room, one would have been mistaken for a mental case should one have informed them that they were spending their last night in a house that had cost them a fortune to build and furnish.

"Baba Nuru, did you attend the meeting organized by Prof Pius, our parliamentary representative?" Mrs. Ntendo asked as she caressed their fat cat that had just leaped on her laps

"I didn't find time. I've been drafting a report that will be emailed to the ministry of youth affairs tomorrow. Hardly anything good comes out of our politicians. They're experts in fighting for superiority and looting public funds."

"I didn't attend the meeting too, but Joy updated me on everything that transpired. Apparently, our parliamentary representative has declared war on us, the Buba people."

"What are you saying, mama Nuru?"

"Don't quote me wrong. Joy told me that Prof Pius is blaming the vice president for his suspension from the cabinet. Prof Pius alleged that the vice president is collaborating with his tribemates to kill the Jaiti people politically. Therefore, he has declared war on us, the Buba."

"Isn't Prof Pius a holder of an honorary doctorate degree in peace from Taifa University? Isn't he the one who's been preaching peace behind T.V cameras?" asked Mr. Ntendo with a slight tremor in his voice.

"Fifteen people have lost their lives, and scores seriously injured in a blood-letting bout of ethnic violence that many are describing as 'politically motivated.' We are now joined by our senior journalist, Violet, reporting live from Banda constituency. Viewers are hereby warned that the following news coverage contains disturbing images."

Mrs. Ntendo switched off the television set.

Rattling noises were heard outside, compelling Mr. Ntendo to walk to the balcony. The security lights were on, illuminating beds of roses, a wooden kennel at the gate, and a well-trimmed Kei-apple fence. Dogs barked on the ground floor, next to the garage.

"Something must be going amiss somewhere," Mr. Ntendo gasped.

Anxiety forced him to rush downstairs.

The horrendous sight that greeted Mr. Ntendo deflated his sanity. His hands flew to his head. Instead of screaming, he laughed—a hopeless, helpless laughter. The garage was in flames. That meant his double cabin pick-up and motor spare parts would be no more.

"No!" He cried after regaining his senses.

Three masked men emerged from the backyard.

"You can't do this to me," screamed Mr. Ntendo.

"That's just the tip of the iceberg," muttered the first man as he sprayed petrol round the mansion.

He tried to stop the first man but was given a kick to the belly that sent him sprawling. Alarmed by her husband's groans, Mrs. Ntendo ran downstairs screaming, carrying her one-year-old son on her back.

"My husband has been killed," she cried.

"Stop!" The second man barked, barring her from getting closer to her injured husband.

"That's not fair."

"Woman, do you mind shutting up?" shouted the third man in a husky monotonous voice—unmistakably that of Yekobo, their security guard.

"Yekobo, how did we wrong you to deserve such a cruel punishment?" she asked, struggling to restrain herself from detonating the bomb of curses in her mouth.

He laughed and said, "That awkward moment when your slave turns out to be your master."

Mrs. Ntendo shot an accusing glance at him. She was about to pounce at the beastly figure before her but surrendered. The huge flames eating up their mansion exaggerated his appearance. The bristles on the man's mask looked like a mane. His eyes, gaping from the mask's tiny holes, glowed green-grey like those of a lion.

The second man saw the angry but helpless look in Mrs. Ntendo's eyes. For that reason, he guffawed and said, "You vowed to wage war against our member of parliament and the Jaiti people, then expect to live peacefully in our land? That can't work. All the Buba must be banished from Jaiti land."

Yekobo moved close to Mrs. Ntendo. He snatched Nuru from her and held him up in the air, head facing the ground.

"This is the devil's offspring. It must be killed before it develops deadly fangs."

Nuru's mother engaged him in a tussle that earned her a stab on the neck before she grabbed her son from him and fled, unaware of her destination. Nuru's life topped her priority list.

"We survived, son," she said forcing a smile, "Unfortunately, your father was critically injured by our assailants. He was hospitalized for two years. He lost his job under mysterious circumstances. Twenty years down the line, he has never landed on a formal job. All his academic testimonials were burnt in our house. Nuru, my only son, my source of inspiration, that's how we were kicked out of Banda. That's how we were reduced to paupers. That's how I got this scar."

"We, the ordinary citizens, should bear the burden of blame. We are our own worst enemies. We've accepted to be brainwashed by the so-called political elites. Little do we know that politicians are multi-faceted. They party, dine, and wine in five-star hotels, but whenever they're faced with any challenge, they incite us to fight each other."

"By the way, the campaign trail for our M.P will pass through Lakira today. I wonder what he has in store for us apart from his usual empty promises."

"Mum, as long as I live, I will never allow anybody to lie to any citizen of Nchi Republic. I'll stand for unity and love."

"I pray you're not planning to plunge into the dirtiest game on earth. I would rather die than see you in the profession of murderers and liars. Politicians are a disgrace to their mothers," said Mrs. Ntendo as she left the room.

"Nuru tried to stand up, but anger and bitterness had paralyzed him. He realized that his body was quivering. Fury continued to build a home in him rapidly. Something needed to be done before rage colonized his body and senses. Nuru knew the remedy was writing. A pen and paper were on a table beside his bed- a replica of his room in Kilimanjaro Hostel. He felt like a committed slave to a pen and paper. That morning, Nuru promptly responded to the orders of his masters. He vented his anger in writing:

"The Intellect! Are You?
This is your ideology
The ideology of turns
Turns to eat and eat
To eat and eat until you get tired
The intellect! Are you?
Inspiring schism
Nurturing tribalism
Trashing nationalism
Leading in incitement
Liberating inter-tribal hatred
Energizing hooligans
Creating rifts
The intellect! Are you?"

C H A P T E R

3

The rugged weather-beaten road that connected Lakira village to Feriani city screeched in pain and surprise, releasing a cloud of brown tears as a strange burden of metals trod on her delicate back, strictly designed for donkey-drawn carts, wheel barrows, motorcycles, and bicycles.

Honourable Salim's motorcade snaked past the cheering crowd. A horde of women ululated and shook their waists vigorously as the convoy of state-of-the-art vehicles moved past them. A dozen farmers in grubby and tattered clothes could not resist the urge to welcome their parliamentary representative in style. They screamed and whistled melodiously. The head teacher of Topeni Primary School stood still next to Nuru, perhaps skeptical of the events unfolding before him, but a bright smile dancing on his lips showed approval of his loyalty to Honourable Salim.

Three young men tried to cross the impenetrable border separating them from the convoy of high-profile personalities and engage their "servant" (as honourable

Salim referred to himself during political rallies) in a greeting ceremony. However, the three young men found themselves at the mercy of the officers' batons. They were beaten up, insulted, and warned never to attempt indulging in a criminal offence of that calibre again. Village elders shook their heads in disapproval of the young men's weird deed. Nonetheless, none among the journalists present at the scene captured the incident.

"What has happened to the new breed of media personalities? Have they abandoned their motto that states 'If it bleeds, it leads?' " Wondered Nuru.

Honourable Salim dragged his bursting body out of his limousine. He remained calm for a minute, trying to comprehend the sea of low-life citizens before him—cheering him and struggling to cross the wide gap (guarded by police officers) and exchange formal greetings with him. He removed his expensive sunglasses, rubbed his eyes, cleared his throat, and said, "I salute you my brothers and sisters, sons and daughters of our beautiful Lakira village."

In response, his constituents ululated. After all, wasn't it sane to welcome a son lost in a faraway land in pomp and glamour? The last time Honourable Salim had been in Lakira village was exactly five years ago while on his mission for greatness. He had promised Lakira villagers and other dwellers of Goba constituency a coffee factory, a stadium, and piped water, but none of his promises were fulfilled. Two days after being declared the new parliamentary representative for Goba, he disappeared into a luxurious residential estate in Feriani city, where he dwelt, dined, walked, and worked with the mighty and great.

There he was again, on the same platform that he stood exactly five years ago, albeit raised higher and covered with a red carpet. A nine-man band of folk singers commonly referred to as the Stars Youth Band moved before the microphone, below the platform. One of the singers played an eight-stringed African traditional musical instrument that was painted red, matching perfectly with red cowry shells on their black shirts.

"Salim o our king
Salim this is your song
Salim the reason we are strong
Salim the reason we shall sing and sing
Viva Salim viva Salim"

Everybody sang along the Stars Youth Band as if it were a national anthem. Honourable Salim moved down the stairs, shaking his obese body to the rhythm of the song. He slapped each of the nine men with a 1000 Nchi shilling note, then returned to his rightful position: the dais. As he removed one of the microphones from its holder, Salim accidentally knocked a few microphones bearing the names of some of the first-rate media houses in Nchi republic. He held the microphone close to his lips and said, "Thank you very much, my brothers and sisters . . . Crocodile?"

"High. High," the crowd responded as they shook their clenched fists in the air in accordance with Honourable Salim's party, New Dawn, official salutation.

"Today is a crucial day of reckoning, my dear brethren. This is my last day to remind you that one of your clansmen is still in the race for the parliamentary seat of Goba constituency. I beg you to forget about Nyilo, my opponent. He's a bastard. We can't account for his ancestral roots. Noble sons and daughters of sweet Lakira village, do you want to tell me that our men are not worth the salt to sire intelligent children?"

"No!" the crowd roared.

"Then here is your son, your brother. In the name of Salim, please vote for me. The fresh blood of the Buba people in me keeps on reminding me that I have to repair this road, establish more job opportunities, build more schools, and construct an international airport in this constituency. Guess what? Lakira village is the place where the airport shall be established.

"Our elders say, 'united we stand, divided we fall.' My kinsmen, since you have proven to everybody that the Wanine clan members are always united by fighting for me in season and out of season; in darkness and light; in happiness and sorrow, I have beautiful tokens for everybody here. They will be distributed to you at the end of our meeting. Last but not least, don't forget to vote for your own blood and flesh, Salim. Thank you."

Nuru watered kale seedlings growing in rows on their kitchen vegetable garden. He tried hard to forget the story behind the dark scar on his mother's neck, but it kept on haunting him.

He sighed and said to himself, "Yes, I have an idea. I'll discuss this issue with my friends through Zoom."

He stuffed his left hand into his breast pocket and searched. His palm touched a crispy material. Nuru pulled it out. It was Amani's passport-size photograph portraying her distinctive facial features: sleepy eyes relaxing below tapered eyebrows, Nubian nose, edgy cheekbones and full pink lips. He stared at it for almost a minute. Her image motivated him to reach for his phone in his pocket. There was no new message from her.

He quickly composed a WhatsApp message on his phone:

"*Hi buddies. I have an idea. I don't know if you'll buy it. I'd like us to form a club that advocates peace and unity in Taifa University and Nchi republic. We may call it Shiners or any other name that you may suggest. In an hour's time, I'll be holding a meeting with you guys via Zoom.*"

He sent it to all his close friends including Amani.

A few seconds later, a WhatsApp message popped into his phone. It was from Derrick: "*Hello, buddy. Thanks for coming up with a brilliant idea of forming Shiners Organization. See you tomorrow on campus. LOL. Are you even aware that the university shall reopen tomorrow? It's not a hoax. Here below is a link to the online version of 'The Daily Wave' newspaper with all the details.*"

Mrs. Ntendo had been watching her son secretly. She walked towards Nuru and snatched away Amani's photo from him.

"Who's this woman?" she howled.

"That's Amani."

"Amani?"

"Yes, a very close friend of mine."

"From which ethnic group?"

"She's a Hazunda."

"Oh my God! Nuru, do you want to die young?

"Mum, please stop it."

"Stop what, my son? Have you grown horns on your head? Since when did you gain authority to exchange words with me?"

"What is the commotion all about?" asked Mr. Ntendo as he walked out of the house.

"Baba Nuru, our son is dating a Hazunda woman."

"Is there anything wrong with that?"

Nuru's mother became so infuriated that she ran into the kitchen screaming at the top of her voice, "My son will never marry a Hazunda woman. A thief! Not over my dead body!"

C H A P T E R

4

An Africa Safari bus came to a halt at Feriani's country bus terminus. The four- hour journey to the city had finally come to an end. Nuru unbuckled his seatbelt, yanked himself up, clutched his suitcase, and shuffled from the bus. He was welcomed by the hustles and bustles of the city. Hawkers hunted and pounced at potential customers and persuaded them to buy their wares. Bus conductors shouted at the top of their voices in a bid to attract commuters despite the rules put in place by the national environmental commission that prohibited shouting. City council officers lurked everywhere like cobras in a ready- to-strike poise. Their brightly coloured but scary uniforms bore a statement that read "I DON'T TOLERATE CORRUPTION." Traffic jam was still conspicuous, notwithstanding the countless strategies put in place by the city council to decongest the city—the latest one being to triple the parking fees for vehicles.

Feriani city had not changed, apart from the increased number of Chinese men supervising various construction projects. Traffic lights turned green. A sea of pedestrians crossed the road. A city council officer, part of the crowd, confronted a young lady.

"Madam, why were you receiving a call while crossing the road?"

"It is my right," she answered.

"So, it is your right to break the city by- law."

"Where is it written that receiving a call is a crime, you corrupt bloody officer?" She screamed.

The young lady was handcuffed and whisked into a waiting land rover.

"Good afternoon, my grandson," An old woman greeted Nuru.

Her tiny face was partially hidden in a white head scarf that spread from her eyebrows to her drooping shoulders. Her left hand was planted on her head, perhaps to prevent the scarf from falling off.

"Good afternoon, grandma," responded Nuru, a quizzical look on his face.

"You look familiar to me. Where have we met before?"

"I beg your pardon, grandma. I don't know you."

"I think I met you somewhere in the countryside . . . that is in . . . It was on . . . well, could you please remind me of your ancestral rural home?"

"I hail from Lakira village."

"Lakira village? Wow!" The elderly woman grinned then continued, "I think that is where I met you, child of my children. Lakira is my ancestral home. Yes! Our ancestral home. Are you a Buba?"

"You guessed right, granny."

"This is not a matter of gazing and guessing. It's instinctive. We, the Buba elders, have an intuition that helps us to identify our tribesmen and women anywhere. It's a unique gift. You won't find it elsewhere. It's the greatest legacy that our ancestors bequeathed us. By the way, what is the name of your clan?"

"Wanine clan."

"I knew my intuitions can never fail me. My grandson, we are from the same clan. I'm the third generation of our great grandfather famously known as Ulekani Kengi. I'm called Mama Nzuina, and you?"

"Nuru Ntendo."

"Praise be to God. He never lets his people down."

Nuru was dumbfounded with surprise.

"Son of my son, I might literally sound like a lunatic, but I'm not one. It's the power of God that has filled me with joy."

"Really?"

"Nuru, your name means 'light.' It is derived from Kiswahili, the language of East Africans. You are a Christian and I know you believe in miracles, don't you?"

"Yes, I do, though occasionally."

"Ten minutes ago, a smartly dressed crook snatched away my second-hand hand bag containing all my possessions. I was stranded, but Jehovah has performed a miracle. He has sent an angel, my clans mate, in my hour of need. Thanks be to God."

"Where are you heading to?"

"My son's place in Northland estate."

Nuru knew that the city was awash with people from all walks of life. Those who pimped to survive, those who conned to win a coin, and those who were easily duped. He scrutinized the old woman's small frail frame and empathized with her.

"Why should one punish such an elderly woman?" Nuru wondered.

He opened his wallet and removed a one-thousand-shilling note, which he handed to the aged woman. She received the note with her two hands and thanked Nuru.

He bade Mama Nzuina farewell and walked towards the bus station, two streets away. A White woman was ahead of him, walking at an equally fast speed. She turned back and their eyes met. Fear was scribbled all over her face. She tucked her clutch bag under her armpit. She too seemed to be on her way to the bus station, but Nuru's close proximity to her made her uncomfortable. The lady held her handset cautiously and aired her tension in French, *"Hi, sweetheart. I'm still in Africa. Living in Africa is the scariest thing. Africa is a safe haven for all the world's deadliest diseases and criminals. I'm scared. There is a thief following me closely."*

Nuru understood French. A strong desire to tell her off seized him, but he held his tongue and walked past her. He had read stories of White Americans calling police officers at the sight of harmless Black men. Cases of White officers shooting unarmed Black people in the US were on the rise too. However, it had never occurred to him that he would be the latest victim of racism in an African country.

"Racism should be declared a mental illness," Nuru said under his breath as he boarded a taxi to Taifa University.

Before he sat down, a hawker pushed an array of headphones into his face. "One costs only two hundred shillings," she said.

Nuru ignored her, but she pressed on. He closed the window. That didn't deter her. She started knocking on the window for almost two minutes, imploring him to purchase one headphone at a discount price.

"I'm not interested," Nuru said as he transferred his attention to an old lady who had just entered the taxi. She was signaling the passengers to remain silent.

"My dear brothers and sisters in Jesus Christ, I greet you," she said.

Her voice sounded familiar. He studied her deep-set eyes. She was Mama Nzuina. Nuru remembered giving her one thousand shillings for fare to Southland estate. She continued, "If you have a human heart, please lend me your ears. The bottom of my world is on the verge of collapsing. My life is falling apart. I'm a widow, robbed of all my children by violence and rendered homeless. I used to own large tracts of land in eastern Democratic Republic of Congo, but one day . . ." She broke down sobbing. "My homestead was turned into a war field for rival militia groups. My husband and all my children were killed. I managed to escape narrowly. I wondered why God had forsaken me. How I found my way into Nchi is a riddle that I'm yet to unravel. Right now, I'm in dire need of your assistance. Please, if you have anything, even a cent, kindly assist me."

Emotional ladies were unable to restrain tears from flowing from their eyes. Many passengers were touched by her story. They gave her money.

Nuru almost screamed, "Con lady!" but who would listen to him? Mama Nzuina was an elderly person. Who had ever heard of an aged woman conning? Wouldn't that be bizarre? He directed his thoughts to the heavy traffic jam.

Vehicles followed each other bumper to bumper. A bunch of street urchins took advantage of the jam and snatched phones from commuters through open taxi windows. Dark grey cumulus clouds hung precariously above skyscrapers that towered over Feriani city.

"Today is on Friday, no wonder the traffic jam is heavier than usual," said a middle-aged man sitting adjacent to Nuru.

"It's sickening," Nuru agreed.

"It's very bad, indeed. I see rains are almost falling, which means that fare will be hiked without warning."

The driver drove the taxi carelessly out of its lane and passed three vehicles. A lady driving a Toyota Forester peeped out of her car's window and tongue lashed the taxi driver. The taxi driver unleashed obscene insults at her.

C H A P T E R

5

*C*ampaign posters of various sizes and shapes dotted walls, pavements, benches, and trees all over Taifa University. The atmosphere bore the smell, taste, and sound of politics.

The students' centre was calm save for the low grumbles of drunk students and the voice of a commentator emerging from a sixty-inch android television mounted on the wall. A big football match between Manchester United and Arsenal F.C, English football clubs with the largest number of die-hard fans in Nchi republic, was being transmitted live. Cases of either Arsenal or Manchester United fans taking their lives on waking to the bitter truth that their team had been thrashed by a team they despised was as common as corrupt politicians and tribalism in Nchi Republic.

Nuru sat at the back of the hall. He was not a football fan. His mission that night was to mine raw materials for his creative writing project.

Cigarette smoke coupled with cheap whisky smell and sweat concocted an acrid smell that could easily formulate a strong anti-mosquito insecticide. Despite the nauseating stench, sneezing in that hall during a big match could earn one a ruthless beating of a snake in a police station. Glasses and bottles of beer cracked nonstop. Match sticks too were lighted while drunkards growled and snored, but nobody complained.

"Goal!" Arsenal fans screamed as they tossed glasses.

"Which team has won?" a lady sitting beside Nuru asked her boyfriend.

He ignored her question.

"That was a perfect maiden score by Arsenal's striker," the commentator remarked. "Hasn't he answered your question? Winners will be known at the end of the match," he said to his girlfriend.

"That is an offside score," a drunk student commented.

"The coach has bribed the referee," a Manchester United fan said as he ran towards the television cage.

He unplugged the TV power cord from the extension cable and screamed, "Come and beat me."

A cacophony of curses and cheers followed his bizarre action. Fed up with the rogue fan's unruly behaviour, two Arsenal fans who were sitting in front approached the Manchester United fan and tried to persuade him to reconnect the TV power cord to the electrical outlet. He responded by firing innumerable insults at them.

They did not take his insults lightly. He was slapped and head-butted, but his wild tongue refused to be tamed. The two Arsenal fans stripped him of his jersey and tore it- an action that charged the fury of many Manchester United fans in the hall. They felt humiliated.

Nuru remained silent, aware of the dire consequences of raising one's voice in such an environment. Glasses and bottles were thrown towards the two Arsenal fans. They stopped harassing the Manchester United fan and took off. However, a stone directed towards one of the violent Arsenal fans missed him and landed on the TV, breaking the screen into small pieces. The blame was swiftly shifted to all Manchester United fans. This formed a foundation for chaos. Football fans begun to physically accost their rivals at the slightest verbal provocation.

Nuru felt insecure. He glanced at his phone. It was already 8:10 pm. There were seven missed calls from Amani. Shiners Organization debut meeting was to be held in his room at 8pm. He had not only left Amani in his house to receive the guests but also promised to return before 8pm.

"Hi, I'm on my way," Nuru texted Amani as he rushed out of the hall. Outside, the noise of angry fans was drowned by melodious voices of Christian Union praise and worship team, in the university chapel, adjacent to the students' centre. He ran upstairs. By the time Nuru reached at the door of his room, he was panting. The door was ajar. He pushed it cautiously. To his surprise, all the invited guests were present.

"Hey, Nuru. You look like a lost he-goat," observed Derrick.

Nuru flashed a fake smile and said, "My utmost apologies for coming late. The writer in me got lost in an eavesdropping mission at the students' centre. I was knocked back to reality when violence erupted."

"Has the situation been dealt with accordingly?" asked Derrick.

"I left when Arsenal and Man-United fans were battling each other mercilessly. I hope all will be well," he said as he squeezed himself next to Amani.

Amani jerked sideways, turned and peered into Nuru's eyes. Derrick whistled. All the other guests laughed. Nuru shook his head. Amani smiled and said, "This guy is pretending to be a guest in his room. Start making formal introductions."

"Introduce us to your queen," said Derrick.

"So you've been seating here like cabbages? You didn't have the courage to talk to each other? Cheer up, guys," said Nuru before clapping his hands.

Derrick stood and said, "We're two against you. The majority will always have their way. Make the introductions. Your tongue won't get torn."

Nuru swiped his left palm under his nose then said, "Well, you win. Let me have the pleasure to introduce naughty Derrick from the school of Computing and Informatics; Allan and Ian from the school of Laws; Beryl and Stacy from the school of Engineering; Nancy from the school of Journalism, and finally Amani and I from the school of Arts."

"I am pleased to be part of this brilliant team. We had the talk via Zoom but this is the moment to walk the talk," remarked Ian.

"Absolutely, Ian. We have just arrived on campus after a short break caused by a violent demonstration whose root cause was tribalism," said Nancy.

"Friends, as I had suggested earlier, we have to form an organization whose main concern will be to heal the wounds caused by tribalism and foster unity not only among students in Taifa University but also in our respective villages and estates," said Nuru

"Nuru, you must become our chairperson," shouted Allan.

"Allan, I beg to differ with you. I think all of us must be leaders in various capacities. I may act as the team leader under the members' consent."

"We declare you our team leader," screamed Allan before being joined by other members.

"Thank you. I humbly accept your choice."

"What are your plans, team leader?" Amani asked.

"I'll be facilitating our meetings, spearheading our activities and also follow the right channel to ensure that our organization is officially registered by the university registrar and the national registrar of clubs and societies."

"What title should we give our organization?" Beryl asked.

"Shiners as Nuru had suggested earlier," said Derrick as he sat at the edge of Nuru's bed.

"Are we all in agreement?" Nuru inquired.

"Yes!" they chorused."

"I will form Shiners WhatsApp Group before midnight. Most of our meetings will be held virtually," said Nuru before pointing to Amani who had raised her hand.

She cleared her throat and announced rather than spoke in an over-rehearsed tone, "There is a mysterious feeling sitting in the heart of my heart. An emotion that has refused to let go of me. It pinches me. It stings me. I try hard not to think about it but it beats my head and bites my heart. I guess this is the right time and place for me to talk about it."

"Go ahead, girl," said Derrick.

"Thank you, Derrick. I have a strong feeling that I must contest for gender affairs secretary."

"You already have my vote," shouted Nuru.

"Mine too," said Derrick.

"But what inspires you?"

"Feminism. I'm an inborn feminist."

"Hoping you're not going to dump Nuru soon," Ian interrupted her.

"Of course I'm not the stereotypical man-hating feminist. I am a woman who thinks men and women rights should be treated as human rights."

"Why can't you call yourself a humanist? I think 'feminist' sounds sexist," said Ian.

"Never. Women have been and still are victims of 'he story.' History, religion, language and nature are currently carrying out a gendercide against women."

"That's an overstatement, Amani. Here in Taifa University, female scholars are enjoying equal rights and privileges as their male counterparts. Moreover, the university admission cut off points for female students are slightly lower compared to male students."

"You forget very fast, Ian. Many female student politicians were sexually assaulted last year while campaigning. Reason? They are just women. Apart from that, what is the ratio of male to female in schools, universities and the national parliament?"

"Feminism lost its relevance in the twentieth century. Anyway, I will vote for you because you are my friend," said Ian.

"Don't vote for me simply because we are friends. Vote for me because you believe in the power of gender equality. Vote for me because you believe male and female lives matter."

When the guests left, Nuru unmuted his music system. Eddy Kenzo's hit song 'Tweyagale' played full blast. He rose and calmly grabbed Amani's hand.

"It is an abomination to remain seated when good music is playing," he said.

Amani laughed and said, "I swear, tonight I must fracture my bones while dancing."

C H A P T E R

6

𝒩uru lay on the lounge by Taifa University's Olympic-size swimming pool. The afternoon sun shone on his semi-nude body, making it a shade darker. He turned the volume of his phone to maximum. Congolese Rhumba music did magic in massaging his soul.

Soft palms suddenly patted him on the shoulders. Nuru pulled the earphones from his ears and raised his head. Beryl was clad in a pink swimsuit that accentuated her curvy body.

"Hi, Nuru. Where's Amani? The two of you rarely give each other space," said Beryl.

"She's designing her campaign posters. She'll be here anytime now."

"Why don't you give her a helping hand? They say many hands make work light."

"I'm not good when it comes to designing."

"Sunbathing is also good for your health. Would you like to join me for a swim?"

"Why not, Beryl?" Nuru said as he rose from the lounge.

He stowed his phone and earphone in his small sports back pack.

"Did you watch the last episode of '*Dark Alley Bitch*' yesterday?" Asked Beryl.

"Soap operas are a female affair. I don't watch them. "

"You never cease to amuse me, Nuru. Time and seasons are changing. Trends too are changing. These days, many women are ardent fans of football and action movies. Similarly, quite a large number of men fancy soaps and wedding shows."

"What I've told you, Beryl, is the reality on the ground. Whatever you're telling me is a baseless theory. By the way, I'm about to start campaigning against soaps."

"Why? Soaps are entertaining and very educative."

"Soaps are spoiling our girls. They're giving them unrealistic expectations about love life."

"Women want to be showered with love. Real love."

"Cool. Thank you for reminding me that women need to be loved. Real love isn't all about imitating the West. It means being realistic. Nuru Ntendo can never be an Alehandro."

Black, brown, and white-skinned bodies splashed water in the swimming pool of Taifa University.

"We have no time to take a quick shower, do we?" Beryl inquired.

"No, we don't. Who said it's compulsory to do so before swimming?"

The two dove into the pool. Nuru swam backstroke while Beryl swam butterfly style.

"Can you swim backstroke, Beryl?"

"I've never tried. I just hate that style with a passion."

"It's one of the most pleasant styles of swimming. Let me show you. "

"But Mr. Teacher, I haven't brought my notebook to jot down critical points," remarked Beryl jokingly.

"These are the instructions."

"Go ahead, Mr. Teacher."

"I've stretched my arms beneath the water surface. All you have to do is lie on them while facing upwards. For your information, you won't stay still on my arms like a rock. You have to move your limbs. Here we go. One, two, three . . ."

Beryl did as she was instructed. After ten seconds, Nuru released Beryl from his arms. She floated for a few seconds, then sunk partially. Nuru assisted her to her feet as she gasped for breath.

"Hello, someone's daughter was about to knock on heaven's door," said Nuru.

"To hell with your style," Beryl surrendered before breaking into loud laughter.

"Practice makes perfect."

"No, Nuru. I'm too young to hug my ancestors."

"Fear not, girl. Be strong."

Beryl didn't respond. She stood still and pouted her lips. Anger was boldly written on her face.

"Have I offended you, Beryl?" Nuru voiced his concern.

"No, look at that dude staring at us over there," said Beryl while pointing a finger at Julius.

"He's one of my closest friends."

"I was about to ask you how the two of you get along with each other. I mean, you're just incompatible. He's the opposite of you; insensitive and infantile."

"You sound so bitter, Beryl. Did he hit you and run?"

"Abomination! He has been trying to woo me, but I'm too big for him. He's like a private detective hired to keep an eye on me. Wherever I am, he's there, staring at me jealously."

"You mean you just hate him because he's wooing you? It sounds crazy. Doesn't it?" Wondered Nuru.

"That's not all. Julius has been spreading rumours that I co-own a brothel in the city centre with ten other ladies in third year."

"What! You must be kidding, girl," said Nuru, raising his eyebrows.

"I know it sounds unbelievable. Julius is a real demon in a man's body. He has slandered me and hurt my pride."

"Indeed he has hurt your pride. One of the things that I dread most is trying to trash the pride of a woman. Ladies have fierce defense mechanisms reserved for protecting their pride."

"You got it right, Nuru. The strength of a woman is in her pride. Poke it at your own risk," said Beryl.

Julius felt humiliated. He thought Nuru was his closest friend. Why was he dating his girlfriend? No, the girl of his dreams. Why were they holding each other suggestively? Why were they talking while staring at him? Were they gossiping about him?

"The game has just begun and I must prove to them that he who laughs last laughs the loudest," mumbled Julius.

Like a leopard wounded by its prey, Julius slunk away. The scorching sun seemed to be scorning him. A female student waved at him, but the burning rage had blinded him.

"Beryl, Julius looks offended. He's walking away. I must find out what the problem is."

"I advise you not to do so."

"Why?" asked Nuru.

"Because you're not a babysitter."

"Indeed, I'm not a baby sitter and I have no dream of becoming one, but I'm just concerned," said Nuru.

"Concerned about what?" Asked Beryl.

"My friend."

"Come on, Nuru. I'm also your friend, are you not concerned about me?"

Nuru was trapped in a dilemma. He remained silent not knowing what to do.

C H A P T E R

7

$\mathcal{A}$mani and Nuru moved from door to door, campaigning. It was a hectic job that required persistence and a thick skin. Often, one would be heckled, intimidated, and insulted by an unruly crowd. Apparently, that's why politics was for the bold and daring. The soft-spoken, polite, and humble fumble, tumble and crumble— so stated the rogue rule of the jungle that reigned in the doctrine of Taifa University politics. To be a good politician, one had to transform oneself into a trickster. Was Amani really ready for the great transformation?

A group of students could be heard chanting the name of her rival in the basement.

"It all comes at a cost," Amani told Nuru as they walked through the hallway of Mandela hostel.

"Nobody will chant your name unless you intoxicate him with either alcohol or money," said Nuru while knocking on the door of room 506.

A short slender lady opened the door.

"You're welcome."

"Thank you," they chorused.

"Good evening. My name is Nuru."

"I'm Amani."

"And I'm Aisha."

"Nice to meet you, Aisha. I'm vying for gender affairs secretary. I propose to empower the girl child. Many female students shun contesting in the Taifa University Students' Union. Need I say, some of those who attempted in the past have been sexually abused while campaigning, and the culprits walked away unpunished? Ladies must be afforded the same dignity as men," said Amani.

"May I interrupt you, Amani?"

"Yes, please."

"Which tribe are you?"

"I'm a citizen of Nchi Republic," replied Amani.

Aisha mopped her mountainous forehead using a white handkerchief then said, "Before you became a citizen of Nchi, you were from a particular tribe. What is the name of that tribe?"

"Excuse me, Aisha, I humbly request you to refrain from advocating for tribalism. It's the very reason behind the election of corrupt leaders. Why can't we be driven by character, competence, and charisma rather than tribalism? One of the goals of education is education for national unity. That goal will remain a mirage if we continue thinking tribally," said Amani.

Aisha burst into a fit of sarcastic laughter and said, "Stop lying to yourself, young lady. I know you know that Nchi stands for a geographical region in which more than forty tribes live competitively. The root word in Nchi is tribe.

Your tribe is your root. You must talk about tribe before mentioning Nchi because tribe is real and Nchi is imaginary. Once again, I ask, which tribe are you from? I would guess you are either a Gebo or Hazunda as your name and accent suggests."

"Sorry, mentioning my tribal identity in this conversation is irrelevant. I'll tell you my policies and past history as a leader if you won't mind," said Amani, emphasizing the word 'policies.'

"I beg your pardon, madam. History doesn't augur well with my ears. Besides, Hazundas are thieves. Who wants to elect a thief? Kindly, the door is open. Leave my room right now before I lose my temper," she said while pointing at her open door.

Nuru shook his head as he walked out of Aisha's room, Amani trailing behind him. Amani knew pretty well that whoever wants to eat what is ripe must be patient. Determination was therefore top on her priority list. Nuru appeared to be visibly disheartened, but she reminded him that life is a struggle. She knocked on the next door—room 507. A hoarse voice asked them to come in. A lady and a man were sitting on a messy bed.

"Good evening," Amani greeted them.

"What do you want? Are you a politician?" the man asked.

"I'm vying for—"

"Give me money or buy us booze," he cut her short.

"I'll neither buy you beer nor give you money but—"

"I know you're not politicians. You're either pests or lost pets."

He grabbed a can of pesticide and fumigated them. Amani and Nuru fled from room 507.

"Oh my God! This must be the apex of stupidity," said Amani while grimacing.

"Campus is not a convent," replied Nuru.

She shot a glance of disbelief and suspicion at him. "Were Julius allegations facts?" She wondered.

Amani had heard heart-wrenching news countless times in her lifetime, but this one was beyond comprehension.

"Julius, are you speaking the truth?"

"I'm an adult, Amani. I can't lie to you."

She became so vexed that she banged the monitor, causing a bunch of freshly printed campaign posters on the table to scatter all over her room. She moved closer to Julius, scrutinized him, then held his head and shook it hard.

"Tell me, Julius. Did you see my boyfriend cavorting with Beryl?"

"Yes, I saw them with my own eyes at the swimming pool."

"Nuru, why are you cheating on me?"

Amani undid her plaited hair as she tottered to the balcony. She stood there alone, sulky and stranded. Amani felt like diving to death by jumping to the ground floor from the balcony but quickly thought about the destructive nature of suicide. She exclaimed, "My spirit is indestructible!"

Amani held her chin and turned towards north east. A clear rainbow had formed on the horizon. She turned back and faced south-west. The sun, partially hidden in the clouds, emitted golden rays that were turning red.

"I know my boyfriend inside-out. He cannot and will never cheat on me," she said.

Amani gained extra strength and stomped into her room. Julius was still present. His eyes remained fixed on hers. A short-lived silence fell upon the two. She moved three steps forward and cried, "You liar. Get out of my room. Get out!" Her voice was heavy and laden with command.

"I have no ill intention, Amani. If you don't believe what I'm telling you, one day the truth will dawn on you."

"Stop wasting my time. Get out of my room."

"I haven't refused to get out, but don't forget that you are too beautiful and intelligent to be misused by a man."

"Rubbish!" She retorted before punching Julius in the face.

"You hit me, Amani?"

"Yes, I did it, and I'm going to high five your face with a toilet seat."

She spat on him, then held her clenched fist above her head, ready to box him. She released it like a bullet towards Julius's nose, closing her eyes while biting her lower lip, but he ducked and dashed out of her room.

Africa: Our Culture, Our Pride. The theme of Taifa University cultural night was written in bold letters on the walls of Miriam Makeba Multi-purpose Hall. On stage, a group of students from Nigeria and Nchi republic were serenading the audience with Yoruba drums known as *Dun Dun*. Tension and band drums were artistically beaten to produce a varying tone similar to someone talking. The band also performed *waka* music before ushering in a group of Ugandan students to play an ensemble of stringed instruments drawn from various ethnic groups of Uganda: *nanga* and *endongo* from the Baganda, *adeudeu* from the Iteso, *adungu* from the Alur, and *litungu* from the Bagisu. Ugandans too were experts in traditional African music. They left the audience craving for more.

The final group to present Afro music were Kenyan students. They sung their national anthem in Kiswahili, East Africa's lingua franca. Unlike the other two groups, Kenyans presented a Somali choral verse, then performed a *mugithi* song blended with *ohangla* beats but danced with *lipala* and *mwomboko* movements.

"That's phenomenal," remarked Nuru while chewing *jolof* rice.

"Africa has a rich culture," said Amani.

She sipped *ikivuguto*, traditional Rwandan sour milk, from a small gourd before dipping a huge lump of *ugali* into a bowl of steaming Ghanaian groundnut sauce. A cocktail of mouthwatering cuisines from the better part of Africa and the Caribbean islands were being attacked by Taifa University students.

Black curtains hanging above the stage were closed for three minutes then opened, revealing DJ Shifta behind an intricate music system. He scratched his dreadlocks and belted out, "Africa hoyee! Africa hoyee! Africa is going to dance tonight. Shake your body, and punch your hands in the air."

Fluorescent lights were switched off. DJ Shifta's selection of the latest African, Caribbean, and American hit music left revelers in awe.

Nuru and Amani danced smoothly. Twinkling colourful disco lights emphasized the celebratory mood. A sea of students danced together irrespective of their tribes, race, and religion. *'We are all humans.'* That seemed to be the message being conveyed by the dancing bodies.

Idibia's song 'My African Queen' steered Nuru to a greater height.

"Amani, you are my African Queen, the girl of my dreams," he whispered to her.

Amani was confused and wanted to know if Nuru was still faithful to her.

"Nuru, remember the promise we made to each other? The promise that no power shall part us. Please, keep the promise."

"You have already formed an inseparable part in my heart."

As the song reached its climax, the screeching sound was heard, ushering in Rex's song, 'The Devil Is Your Friend.'

"Jah Rastafari," a group of third-year Law students famously known as Ganja Farmers chanted. Their message was clear; they wanted the DJ to play for them roots reggae music.

"If you are a Rasta man, lift your hands in the air and say aireee," the DJ's voice resonated across the hall introducing Richie Spice's song 'The world is a cycle.' So exhilarated was Ryan, the gang leader of Ganja Farmers, that he lit a marijuana stick. He assisted his acquaintances to do the same. They went ahead and begun to do what they described as marijuana smoking contest. A thick cloud of smoke issued from their mouths but nobody appeared perturbed. Amani started coughing uncontrollably.

"Insensitive beings. The security officers are entertaining this crap?" Complained Nuru as he led Amani out of the hall.

"Members of the Rastafarian sect have spoiled the night," cried Amani.

"Those are not Rastafarians but campus crooks."

"Isn't that the Rastafarians' way of life? Don't they smoke weed?" Asked Amani.

"Indeed, Rastafarians smoke marijuana but strictly during their religious ceremonies, not in public places."

"You mean Rastafarians have a defined religious doctrine?"

"Rastafarianism isn't just a religion but a movement. It was started in the 1930's in Kingston, Jamaica, by people of African origin. Right now, it has believers worldwide. Their sacred book is called the Holy Piby. Rastafarians believe that the late emperor Haile Selassie is their Black messiah."

"The former emperor of Ethiopia?" Amani asked.

Nuru nodded and continued, "Emperor Haile Selassie was once interviewed by a Canadian radio station where he described himself as being mortal, but this has never shaken the faith of Rastafarians."

"I guess that's the reason why I've heard many roots reggae musicians paying tribute to Ethiopia and Haile Selassie," observed Amani.

"Rastafarians believe Ethiopia is Zion, their Promised Land. They also believe that all African descendants living outside Africa will return to their ancestral land."

Nuru's phone vibrated. It was a reminder for him to attend Hosanna Night organized by officials of the Christian Union. Cultural night and Hosanna night were always coinciding. Christian Union officials did so intentionally to discourage their members from partying with non-believers.

Amani and Nuru were warmly received by the usher at the entrance to the chapel and directed to two unoccupied seats.

"Praise God, brethren. This evening I'm blessed. My name is Prince Jackson. I'm saved and love Jesus as my personal saviour. Tonight, I urge you to reflect on the great deeds that God has done in our lives. We are living courtesy of his love. Brethren, God's love for us is everlasting. For your information, God himself is love. John 3:16 underscores God's love for humanity. He sent his only begotten son, Jesus Christ, to die on the cross for our sins. Praise God, my brothers and sisters in Christ."

Amani's phone interrupted the sermon with Lucky Dube's song 'One People.' A member of the Christian Union having a secular ringtone on his or her phone was tantamount to an abomination. The whole congregation stared at her with dismay and disgust.

"We bind!" Pastor Prince said, airing his disappointment.

"What is wrong with a secular song that preaches love and harmony?" Whispered Nuru.

The preacher continued, "We, members of the Christian Union, are full of love. That's why our arms are ever open to receive visitors. I understand that tonight God has blessed us with visitors. If you are a visitor, please greet the congregation."

"Praise God. My name is Hope. I'm not a member of the Christian Union, but I feel blessed to celebrate Hosanna Night with you. I'm also vying for the position of vice chairperson in the students' union. I come from southern Nchi, in the county of Mbayuyu people."

Most of the visitors were politicians and they introduced themselves the same way Hope did.

"God is working wonders. He has brought all the politicians to uplift his name. Praise God. I told you that we are still contributing towards the purchase of modern musical instruments for the choir. Our future leaders in the house, if you feel blessed, please assist the choir in making their dream a reality. At the moment, I would like one choir member to lead us in a Mbayuyu praise song. I urge us to dance boastfully to the song, the way the Mbayuyu people do. You know how boastful Mbayuyu people are?"

Amani walked out of the chapel. Nuru followed her.

"That wolf in a sheep's skin has pissed me off," hissed Amani.

"Stop being the first one to cast the stone."

"Nuru, I know it sounds judgmental but we can't evade the truth."

"Which truth?"

"Prince Jackson pegged my former roommate, Alice, then later forced her to procure an abortion. Besides, he's having secret sexual affairs with a chain of campus chicks."

"Why trouble yourself with what he does in secret? Avoid burdening your brilliant mind. Heed his sermons and ignore what you hear about him," said Nuru.

"I won't stop pointing out his hypocrisy."

"I know he has pissed you off. Relax," he said.

Amani responded by rolling her eyes and sneering.

"You look like this...," said Nuru as he made faces at Amani, forcing her to burst into laughter.

"By the way, it's damn cold out here. We better return to the chapel," suggested Nuru.

"No, let's go to your room," insisted Amani.

Three bodies, silhouetted by the security light, appeared to be in a compromising situation. Driven by curiosity, Nuru moved closer to them. Two male students—one tall and the other extremely short—in their final year of study were fighting over Purity, a first-year student. Purity was famous for drinking like a fish, smoking like a coal train, and sleeping with any willing man. '*Women from* Gebo *tribe are always loose,*' rumour mongers emerged with their stereotypic theory.

"Purity, it's either me or that son of a bitch," the tall man screamed.

"Who gave you the right to speak to my girlfriend? Do you have bricks for brains?"

The short man pounced on the tall man's pot belly and bit him. A high-pitched scream confirmed the excruciating pain he was experiencing.

"Please stop the fight," cried Nuru.

He held the short man who was overpowering the tall man. The tall man directed a heavy blow at the short man. Nuru gave him a slight push as the blow landed squarely on the short man's face. The tall man tripped on a stone, staggered for a while, lost balance, and fell on the ground. The short man knew this was an opportune moment to give his opponent the beating of a lifetime, but he couldn't move forward. Nuru was holding his arms tightly. He had to free himself very fast and tackle his enemy. He kicked Nuru on the right knee, but instead of letting him go, Nuru just squeaked and tightened his grip around the short man's leathery hands.

"My friend, don't fight him. Cool down," he pleaded, addressing the short man.

"Corporal, this is the man we were asked to extinguish," growled the short man.

"What!" Nuru bellowed.

"Are you not defaming Sylvester, a man of the people with the rubbish you call Shiners?" shouted the short man.

"I'm not a politician."

"But you are a propagandist targeting our boss. Kill him co-corporal," roared the tall man from the ground.

He rose, staggered towards Nuru, and slapped him on the forehead. Nuru tried to shield himself but ended up freeing the short man. The two drunken men managed to tackle him from left and right but he remained firm on the ground.

Since Nuru had been sandwiched by the two men, he used his left hand to push the tall and unstable man while his right hand jostled the stocky man. Amani screamed with the hope of attracting the congregation to save her boyfriend but to no avail. The chapel had sound-proof walls.

Purity walked out, leaving the two men wrestling their mediator. Nuru continued pushing them away from him. Luckily, the tall man fell down again, followed by the short man.

Nuru knew his assailants would recuperate very soon. For that reason, he beckoned Amani, and they tore off to her room.

C H A P T E R

9

Nuru's eyes were red and puffy. His legs were aching. He had swallowed some tablets prescribed to him by the university physician, but the pain refused to be tamed.

"The case is now lying in the hands of the university security officer," he said to Amani as they headed towards Garang Lecture Hall.

Amani felt the weight of pain and bitterness in his voice. She wasn't physically hurt, but her heart bled for Nuru. It was impossible not to empathize with him.

"I 'm so scared the culprits may not be brought to book," remarked Amani, extremely worried.

"I don't give a damn. The university administration is aware that my life is in danger," he responded.

"Last academic year, hooligans of Corporal Squad raped a female student contesting for gender affairs secretary. Furthermore, they've been bullying anybody opposing them. I keep on asking myself, isn't the university aware? If yes, what has it done to let justice take its course? Nuru, can't you smell a rat?"

"Indeed, it's a complex issue but we shouldn't appeal to speculation," said Nuru.

"We must use the power of pen and paper. They say a pen strikes harder than a sword."

"How?"

"Can't you write and post protest poems in Shiners Organization blog?" asked Amani.

"Protest poems? A big no for me. It would be better to continue uploading *peace* poems in that blog."

"Hi, friends," interrupted Julius who was moving in an opposite direction. He continued, "I'm sorry for what happened to you guys last night."

"It's ok. They say a road minus obstacles probably leads you nowhere. We're now sure Shiners is heading somewhere," said Nuru, expressing his optimism.

"By the way, how is your neighbour faring?" Julius asked.

Nuru met his question with a question. "Whose neighbour?"

"Aren't you aware that Rashid was brutally injured by unknown masked hooligans last night?"

"He's such a humble and harmless dude," cried Amani.

"That must be a mistaken identity. I know they were targeting me," said Nuru.

"All will be well, buddies," Julius said as he walked away from them.

Amani and Nuru made their way to Garang Lecture Hall. They were thirty minutes late for the lecture, but the lecturer still had not turned up. Professor Patel, the Caribbean

Literature lecturer, had never reported to work late. Students clustered in small groups outside the lecture hall. A keen observer would have noted that most groups consisted of students from the same ethnic group. Only a handful of foreign students, students from minor tribes and a few from major tribes raised in urban centres mingled freely with various groups. Amani and Nuru sat on a secluded concrete bench overlooking the lecture hall and engaged themselves in a tête-à-tête.

In the middle of their conversation, her phone vibrated.

"Hello. With whom am I speaking?"

"This is the dean of students. Is that Amani, a second-year student of Literature?"

"Yes, sir. How may I help you?"

"The university security officer has informed me that you were harassed last night by hooligans. I would like to see you urgently right now in my office."

"Can I come with another victim of last night's attack?"

"That's not necessary at this stage. Just come alone. It won't take long. Moreover, it's crucial and confidential."

She disconnected the call and heaved a sigh.

"Nuru, the dean would like to see me concerning last night's attack."

"That's good. Let's hope for the best."

"No, hope for the worst."

"You sound so pessimistic, Amani."

"This is Taifa University. A dead university ruled by goons."

Nuru laughed and said, "A dead clock is right twice a day."

"That's exactly what I'm going to find out. Meanwhile, answer my phone for the moment. I'll keep you updated on everything that transpires. Bye! I'll miss your company."

Amani walked with her usual aura of confidence. Her nose up in the air, shoulders hunched backwards and feet doing the work, walking in short calculated steps.

Amani's phone buzzed. The screen read, "My Sweet Mum calling." Nuru was hesitant to receive the call. He was tempted to end the call and switch off the phone, but wouldn't that be rude? Hadn't Amani already formed an inseparable part of him?

"Hallo, mum. This is Nuru, Amani's friend."

"Nuru who?"

"Ntendo."

"Have you stolen my daughter's phone?"

"No, please. I'm afraid Amani is quite far. She left her phone with me."

"Who are you to her?"

"I'm her friend!"

"You're just friends?"

"Yes."

"May it be so."

"Why are you so worried, mum?"

"I must be worried for my daughter because she's interacting with a man from the wrong tribe."

"What do you mean?"

"I mean what I say."

"But mum."

"Shut up! Don't dare call me mum, you shameless Buba man." She disconnected the call.

Lush vibrant grass formed a carpet under Nuru's feet. It appeared to be growing stronger and greener every minute in spite of being trodden by thousands of feet. Nuru's bunch of keys slipped from his quivering hand and fell beneath the bench through a big crack close to the edge. He got down on his knees to retrieve them. As he reached for his keys, Nuru realized that tufts of grass growing beneath the bench were weak and yellow in colour. Were they not safe from the harsh elements of weather and nature? Didn't they receive enough rainwater and nutrients from the soil like other plants growing on an exposed ground? What caused the disparity? He stashed the bunch of keys into his pocket and resumed his sitting position on the bench. The sun was already overhead. He looked up to the sky and was almost blinded by the shining sun. He smiled and mumbled, "Now I know why tufts of grass beneath the bench are yellow and weak."

Students were still scattered everywhere in small tribal groups. Three different campaigners gave him flyers for politicians eyeing various seats in the students' union. It was a known fact that a few months preceding elections in Taifa University were rich seasons of harvest. One was assured of free beer, soda, and money as long as one acted as a campaigner, hooligan or attended a political rally.

Nuru analyzed the content of each campaign leaflet. Surprisingly, they had striking similarities: too many words with negligible or zero ideological content.

"What a bunch of educated zombies!" He mumbled while dumping the leaflets in a dustbin beside the bench. Nuru had sat there for almost thirty minutes. He stood up, stretched and yawned. That is the moment his eyes landed on a troubled figure approaching him. It was Amani. She looked sullen and worn out. He froze: mouth agape, hands outstretched.

"Are you alright, Amani?" Inquired Nuru.

"I have slapped the Dean of Students. That beast is not worth his title," said Amani as she neared him. Nuru walked towards Amani and placed his right hand over her shoulders. He then walked with her back to the concrete bench.

What exactly happened?" Nuru asked, his sonorous voice laced with love and fear.

"He promised that he would take action against members of Corporal Squad on condition that I slept with him. He also promised me a First Class Honour's Degree if I became his committed side chick. I laughed at his awkward idea. That's what made him to attempt grabbing my boobs forcibly. I blocked his hand with my left elbow and served him a sudden hot slap on his face with my right hand. His glasses are in pieces. I dashed out of his office, leaving him swearing to teach me a lesson if I expose him."

"Did he do anything else?"

"No, I am just scared that I might have destroyed his eyes. His threats too should not be taken lightly. He may decide to mutilate my grades."

"I don't think your slap can uproot his eyeballs. You fought like a real warrior by ambushing him with a slap. Were it not for your courage, you would have been the latest victim of sexual assault in Taifa University."

"What of the threats?" Amani asked in a more relaxed tone.

"Those were kicks of a dying horse. He thought you were a fragile helpless chick that could be easily manipulated sexually. The sudden electric slap proved him wrong. Toxic masculinity programmed him to threaten you, for him to sound manly," said Nuru.

Amani fluffed her short hair and said, "He rattled a female cobra. The shameless old dude will never mess up with people's daughters."

"You are my heroine," said Nuru as he hugged her.

"Did anyone call me?" She asked.

"Only your mum," replied Nuru.

"Did you receive?"

"Yes, but she was very mad at me after telling her my second name."

"I know she'll eat my liver. She has warned me many times against associating with people from the Buba tribe."

"Don't be worried, Amani."

"We must be worried, Nuru. My mum is capable of ruining our relationship."

"Amani, we are sailing on the same boat. My mum once caught me admiring your photograph. She asked me about your tribe. I told her that you are a Hazunda, and that was enough to make her rebuke me. I expected my father to react more explosively, but to my amazement, he didn't find any fault in his son dating a Hazunda."

"I wish my father was around," said Amani

"Where is he?"

Amani rolled her eyes. She felt her story was too disgraceful to be shared with anybody.

"*Nuru is neither 'anybody' nor 'somebody' but a part of me,*" she thought.

"Growing up with a father figure who'd tell me bedtime stories, hold my hand, and sing to me 'Twinkle, Twinkle Little Star' only occurred in dreams."

"I'm sorry. Did your dad pass away when you were a very small kid?"

"According to my mum, my father is alive. I know him physically but not emotionally, thanks to his portrait in my room."

"Where is he?" Asked Nuru

"My mum told me he disappeared mysteriously with a White woman whom he met at a tourism agency where he used to work as a clerk. My mum was the operations manager. At that point, I was only three years old. I really hunger for a biological father figure to bless my marriage, bless my generation, and advise me on issues of marriage and relationship."

"Has your mother made any effort to trace him?"

"She has posted notices in newspapers and reported to the relevant authorities, but her efforts have proven to be useless. Rumour has it that he died abroad. I believe one day I'll smile and speak with my father."

"Do you think your mum can forgive your dad?"

"Yes, my mum has never stopped speaking about my father with passion and nostalgia."

There was a sudden eruption of noise in Garang Lecture Hall. The small groups of students milling around the lecture hall dwindled rapidly, and everyone converged in the hall.

"What could be the cause of that uproar?" Asked Nuru.

"Maybe hooligans are manhandling Professor Patel."

"Let's find out," suggested Nuru.

Aspiring student leaders were standing in a single file in front of the audience. Five male students in muscle shirts that exposed their enormous biceps and chests introduced each politician to the audience in turns. Two of them had leather whips while the rest were armed with clubs. As Nuru and Amani entered the hall, a section of students begun to cheer for them while others jeered. It was like a jeering and cheering competition. Their voices were uniform at first, but after a while, the cheerers overpowered their opponents.

"Nuru! Nuru! Amani!" The audience chorused.

"Please come to the floor, Nuru and Amani," the shabby-looking stage manager said in a calm voice that contrasted with his demeanor.

This came to them unexpectedly. The two joined the rest on the dais, though not knowing what to say. Politicians are widely known for being generous with words. Nuru was the odd one out—a lone activist amidst hooligans and politicians. Perhaps Amani would speak for Shiners Organization and sell her political manifesto, but was that not dangerous to their organization in a university where any club or society having a politician as one of its members was deemed to be politically motivated?

It was therefore necessary for Nuru to warn Amani against speaking for the organization. His eyes quickly darted across the lecture hall. It was brimming with anxious faces. He unfolded his handkerchief, dabbed his face and blew his nose. Nuru turned to Amani and whispered, "Kindly don't talk about Shiners Organization at the moment. I'll do so." Amani remained silent. He repeated his statement in a louder whisper.

Amani just nodded and nudged him. He patted her shoulder gently and said, "Relax."

"I'm annoyed. These stage managers are the goons who almost killed us last night."

"And I'm extremely shocked to learn that you are just annoyed," said Nuru half- jokingly.

The aspiring student leaders all appeared to share the same ideology. They assured everyone that curbing tribalism and corruption would be their first agenda once elected.

The MC, after christening himself "Brother," requested all politicians to shake his hand before addressing the audience. "Handshakes symbolize harmony and friendship," he added.

"Corporal goons have decided to preach peace today? This is awesome," remarked Nuru.

"Don't be fooled. The MC is collecting money in the name of brotherhood handshakes. You must pay him to speak. Have you forgotten that Corporal Squad is the local government on campus?" responded Amani.

"I won't pay him even a cent," vowed Nuru.

"You can say that again," said Amani.

"Ladies and gentlemen, put your hands together for Nuru Ntendo," the MC alerted the audience. Nuru shook his hand.

"Where's the security fee?" He whispered while squeezing Nuru's palm.

"I don't need your protection," Nuru protested. He snatched the microphone from the master of ceremonies. A wild applause confirmed Nuru's popularity and fame.

The MC used his left hand to pinch his right shoulder. Members of Corporal Squad present in the hall quickly decoded his secret message. They all thumped their feet on the floor to pledge their loyalty to their rogue group.

"Comrades united," Nuru screamed.

"Yes, we can," the audience replied.

"No, go away. Who are you?" Members of Corporal Squad grunted.

"I'm sorry. I didn't introduce myself."

"Stop!" The MC cut him short.

"Go ahead," a large section of the audience encouraged Nuru.

Corporal Squad controlled Taifa University with an iron fist. Students who were cheering Nuru did so cautiously, for fear of being tortured.

Amani covered her mouth with her left palm. How would it feel to be humiliated in public? Had they not suffered enough in the hands of Corporal Squad?

"Let it be the way it will be," she cried.

Nuru continued with his speech. "Where there is love?"

"There is harmony," the audience responded.

"Go away," the master of ceremonies said as he snatched the microphone from him.

The five hooligans pushed Nuru to the floor and whipped him.

"Let us strip him," suggested one of the hooligans.

"Before you kill him, kill me first," Amani yelled.

Nuru was a darling to many, thanks to Shiners. Thousands of students hated tribalism. They needed a saviour who would emancipate them from the bondage of tribal segregation. Ironically, many would speak against tribalism in public but later embrace the vice when faced with any fear or challenge. Phrases such as "tribalism is the cancer of development" and "it is our turn to eat" were commonly used at Taifa University and in Nchi Republic.

Scores of brave students made their way to the stage and shielded Nuru from the rain of whips. The MC and his troop tried to penetrate the big wall of Nuru's supporters, but they were thrown from the stage like flies. The audience gained the audacity to celebrate. Nuru was carried shoulder high triumphantly.

"Comrades united!" He screamed.

"Yes, we can!" The students roared.

Members of Corporal Squad, for the first time in the history of Taifa University, were defeated. They left Garang Lecture Hall, one by one, crestfallen.

CHAPTER 10

$\mathcal{A}$mani's campaign posters had been defaced and torn. Offensive words were scribbled on them. She glowered at the notice board.

"This is politics, my dear. A very dirty game," Nuru comforted her. "Not everyone you see on campus is sane. By the way, we are all insane, but the percentage of insanity varies from one individual to another. Perhaps I'm more insane than you."

"The number of educated zombies is skyrocketing at this university," said Amani.

"Cool down. They say every market has a mad person. Taifa University, too, has its share. No wonder their common sense made them do the most sensible thing on your posters."

"You call that common sense?" She inquired while brushing her hair backwards.

"Yes, common sense that's only common among educated zombies."

"I'm glad Corporal goons were disappointed today. The war is officially on—Shiners against Corporal."

"Love triumphed over violence. By the way, I'm scheduled to attend a tribal meeting organized by Tetung students."

"What for?" Amani asked.

"I need to evaluate the severity of tribalism and the effectiveness of Shiners. Have we changed the attitude of Taifa University students towards tribalism? That's the question that's nagging me."

"Don't you think your presence will affect their conduct?"

"All the costumes and props for the Theatre Production course unit are in my room."

"Nuru, please answer my question."

"I thought you are a Literature student. Do you need a microscope to see the answer?"

"Stop being sarcastic."

"I've stopped. Are you happy now?"

"Please, Nuru," she mumbled.

"For sure, my presence may influence their conduct," said Nuru as he scratched his moustache.

"So, why waste your time on a mission that's bound to fail?"

"Because yours truly is a smart Literature student. I will conceal my identity in a cowboy cap, sunglasses, fake sideburns, and a blue suit. Clap for me."

"Brilliant!" Said Amani.

"Didn't I ask you to clap for me? Please follow simple instructions."

Amani threw back her head and laughed before clapping her hands near his ears.

"Thanks. It's now time for me to leave. Please stay in your room. I think it's safer there," said Nuru as he kissed her goodbye.

Nuru entered Miriam Makeba Multi-purpose Hall and occupied a back seat. Members of Tetung Students Association walked into the hall in small groups. After about ten minutes, everybody had settled down. The chairperson of the association was a tall, dark man whose down-to-earth personality had earned him respect among his peers. He asked the DJ to curtain raise the meeting with two Tetung circumcision songs.

The Tetung and Buba were neighbouring communities. Intermarriages between the two communities wasn't strange. Tetung names were frequently used by Buba people and vice versa. Since Buba was a relatively smaller tribe compared to Tetung, many cultural critics termed Buba an endangered language. The most striking trait about the Tetung and Buba was that no tribal animosity had ever been reported between them. Moreover, many Buba could speak Tetung dialects and the Buba language fluently.

"Welcome, my brothers and sisters. Peace be with us," said the chairperson in one of the Tetung dialects.

"Pardon," a few students interrupted.

The Tetung language had more than ten dialects. Mutual intelligibility between certain dialects stood at about twenty percent. The chairperson repeated his statement in English, to the dissatisfaction of students who could comprehend his dialect. During such meetings, English was termed as an imperialist language. The chairperson brought the meeting to order, but low-toned mumbles and grumbles were still audible. He reiterated to his tribemates the persistent plea from their leaders at the national level for the unity of Tetung speakers. It was alleged that speakers of certain dialects distanced themselves from the activities of the tribe and cooperated with 'outsiders.'

"Speakers of our sweet Tetung language, we are aware that in three weeks' time, we shall be having the students' union elections. Similarly, our national elections will take place a day after tomorrow. The riddle that needs to be unraveled tonight is: are we ready for the race? In our midst, we have some of our brothers and sisters who'd like to have a share of the cake on our behalf."

"Where are they?" a female student inquired.

"I beseech all aspiring student leaders to stand wherever they are. How many are they? One, two, three . . . seven, eight. Isn't this a big number? What do you think, friends?"

"Greed breeds grief. Presenting eight candidates would be very greedy of us. If the voting system at Taifa University is anything to go by, then we're in for a very big loss. Nobody can accept to give one tribe all the positions in the students' union. We have to be wise and reduce the number," said Dan, the association's chief advisor.

There was another hand in the air.

"Yes, Clifford."

"Mr. Chair, I think Dan has aired a very critical point. We, the Tetung, can't go alone to the ballot box. We need the support of other tribes. I suggest we form a coalition with the Mbayuyu. Moreover, we need to bag the minorities' votes. It's very simple. We'll nominate one of them to the students' union. I know Hazunda and Gebo students have already formed a coalition, just like their national political leaders, but they can't scare us. Apart from that, we all know that Tetung politicians are among the most divided in Nchi. That's why we're the only major tribe in Nchi lacking a stable tribal chief. I think this is a blessing in disguise. We may consider approaching each bigwig Tetung politician separately and ask for funding in return for our support of his or her quest to be our national tribal chief."

"Thank you, Clifford. Our final-year students will discuss the issue of leadership and political coalition with their counterparts from Mbayuyu tribe and decide who will vie for what. Concerning approaching various politicians for funding, that's a good idea. We'll form a committee that will organize and plan for the visits."

Nuru's phone vibrated. It was his mother. He walked out of the hall to receive the call.

"Hallo, mum. How are you?"

"I'm fine. It's been so long since we talked. How are your studies?"

"Good, as usual."

"Well, do you remember the story I told you concerning the tribal clash that led to our eviction from Banda?"

"It haunts me daily," replied Nuru.

"Son, your mum has a dark scar on her neck to bear witness forever. Some things are just indelible. This is a fact that our government has refused to acknowledge."

"Do we have a government in Nchi? Murderers like Pius and his friends are the beasts running our so-called government. Pius should be rotting somewhere in prison. Instead, he is a cabinet minister," said Nuru.

"We are tired of our unjust society, my son. By the way, I called to inform you that we, the victims of Banda tribal violence, have organized ourselves. We shall hold a peaceful demonstration tomorrow on the streets of Feriani city."

"Isn't it dangerous, mum?" Interrupted Nuru.

"What a stupid question!"

"But Mum, you need to be careful."

"My cowardly son. There you go, lecturing your own mother."

"That was just my opinion. Anyway, remember to pass by our campus. Bye."

11

$\mathcal{G}$ood morning, mum. Welcome to Taifa University. How was your journey?" Said Nuru.

"Who's this woman? Isn't she the Hazunda woman whose photo you were admiring?" Inquired Mrs. Ntendo in Buba language.

"I am coming to that. Amani, meet my mum. Mum, this is Amani, my girlfriend."

"It's a great pleasure to meet you, mum."

Amani extended her right arm towards Mrs. Ntendo.

Instead of shaking Amani's hand, she waved at her. Nuru studied his mother's face. She met his gaze defiantly. Amani, on her side, sandwiched her bowed head between two sweaty palms. In place of joy was apprehension and hatred.

"Will you take coffee, tea, or juice?" Inquired the waiter, breaking the loud silence.

"Three glasses of cocktail juice," ordered Nuru.

"Excuse me, are you going to feed this thief too?" Asked Mrs. Ntendo while pointing at Amani.

"Mum, I'm disappointed in you," clucked Nuru.

"Disappointed in the person who carried you for nine months in her womb? Just because of this woman? I can't stand the sight of this thief. Stay away from my son, woman."

Most eyes of students in the cafeteria were now on them. Embarrassed and enraged, Amani swaggered out of the cafeteria.

"No, don't do that, Amani," pleaded Nuru as he held her hand.

"Don't dare touch me," she screamed and moved on.

Nuru rose from his seat and started following Amani.

"Are you running away from me?" Mrs. Ntendo jabbered.

Nuru stopped suddenly and said, "Mum, why are you torturing my soul?"

"It's you who's torturing my soul, my son."

"You don't understand how I feel towards Amani. She is such a good girl."

"And you don't understand how I feel pity on you. Falling for the wrong tribe? My son, don't be like a horse that thinks of itself a donkey while grazing with donkeys."

"That's a very stereotypical way of thinking."

"As our people say, 'what an elder can see while seated, a young person cannot see even while standing on top of a mountain.' Open your inner eye, and see what I'm revealing to you."

"Sorry for disappointing you, mama. I belong to a brand-new generation. A generation whose inner eyes see beyond tribalism."

The waiter placed three glasses of juice on their table. Nuru didn't ask him to return one glass, for he believed Amani would join them soon or later.

"Nuru, look at this scar. Look at it again and again. It's worth your life and my life. I risked my life to save yours. In return, you despise and disobey me?" she said in a bitter tone while pinching the scar on her neck.

"Mum, I'm not disobeying you but loving for the sake of my heart. Loving to prevent future bruises and injuries. I don't want us to get any more scars. I'm glad the wound on your neck healed successfully many years ago."

"A bearer of a scar—don't think she's healed."

"A scar is a sign of healing," he insisted.

"In my case, it hides a gaping wound that can only be cured by you, son, but you are a big disappointment."

"How does my relationship with Amani hurt you? She's the love of my life."

"So, you won't stop poking my scar?"

"It's true you suffered for my sake. I truly lack the words to express my appreciation."

"Your words do not match with your actions. You have been bewitched," Mrs. Ntendo interrupted.

"Allow me to complete my statement, mum. We can't whine and moan over the past. The time is ripe for us to unchain ourselves from the blunders of history and focus on the prosperity of the present and the future."

"You are becoming more disrespectful. This is very unusual of you!" She screamed as she stood.

"Please, wait mum. Just a minute."

"I'll talk to you after dealing with the person who bewitched you. I know her."

She banged the table and stomped out of the cafeteria.

Nuru took a long sip of juice. The tantalizing juice turned bitter all of a sudden. A horde of students around him, talking about politics from a tribal perspective, looked like deadly vampires grinding their long pointed canine teeth in preparation to suck blood and humanity from any human being, nay, transform anybody into a vampire. Nuru thought of his mother being one of the victims of the vampire's magical venom. For a moment, he visualized himself holding Amani amid millions of hungry and angry vampires.

"Good morning and welcome to our top news headlines."

Everyone in the cafeteria became calm, focusing on the television set.

"The head of state has urged Nchi citizens to maintain peace and order ahead of the country's general election set to be held tomorrow. Victims of the tribal clash that hit Banda constituency two decades ago have vowed to stage a peaceful demonstration on the major streets of Feriani city despite the police commissioner terming it illegal. 'I'm innocent,' says Honourable Professor Pius, one of the suspected masterminds of the tribal violence that hit Banda amid human rights watchdogs' pressure on him to quit politics. For these and many more stories, join us at the top of the hour."

Nuru paid the bill and left. Outside, clouds were scattered and the sun was shining brightly.

From far, he caught sight of Amani's figure perched on a concrete bench in Sankara Garden.

"No!" Nuru exclaimed, blinking his eyes several times. The vision of vampires hit him again. Desperately, he attempted to give her a call but gave up. There was no time to waste. He sprang into motion.

Nuru's loud footsteps startled Amani. She turned to look behind. Their eyes met. His sight nauseated her. She bent forward and struggled to puke. Nothing came out.

"It pains me to see you stressed," said Nuru, placing his hands on Amani's shoulders. He smiled. She sneered.

"I love you, Amani," he said in a low voice.

Amani frowned and said, "I'm afraid, our relationship can't work."

"Amani," he whispered.

"Just stay away from me," she blurted out and brushed his hands off her shoulders.

Silence reigned.

"How can I stay away from you? You're part of me," said Nuru, killing the awkward silence.

She remained motionless. It was difficult to read her emotion. He wrapped her in his hands. She didn't resist. Her body trembled against his own.

"It's me who's in love with you. Forget about my mother's ill attitude towards your tribe."

"Please, I don't want to be a wedge that separates son from mother. Let's just be friend," said Amani.

"You've dumped me? Have you forgotten the promise we made to each other?"

Amani became conscious of her blunder. "I don't know what's entered my brain. I'm just confused," she said, tears glittering in her eyes

"Oh! I understand," cried Nuru as he tightened his grip around her body.

Amani gasped.

"I wish we could remain in this position forever," remarked Nuru.

"Your wish has been granted," said Amani.

His phone's message tone interrupted them.

"I can't let you go at the expense of a cheap message."

"I'll take the phone from your pocket," said Amani.

Amani dug her hand into Nuru's pocket and clutched the phone.

"Read the message please," said Nuru.

"You don't need some privacy?" Inquired Amani.

"That's ridiculous. How can I be afraid of reading my own message? You are me."

The text message read: '*Hi honey, we had a great moment together last weekend. When are we meeting again?*'

"So, it's true you are cheating on me?" Amani screamed before dropping the phone on the ground.

"What's the problem?"

"You are the problem, Mr. Liar," spluttered Amani.

Nuru picked his phone from the ground and read the message. He almost burst with surprise. The number was strange. Moreover, Amani was his only girlfriend.

"Amani, we've haters."

"Whether we have haters or lovers, I call it quits, Mr. Liar."

"I wish you would have understood."

"Understood what? Your lies?"

"I still love you no matter the tides."

"I had only one heart, Nuru. I'm in deep pain you've broken it."

"You can't walk away from me."

"Stop following me. I will embarrass you with slaps," barked Amani.

C H A P T E R
12

Amani's eyes were still heavy with sleep. She had tossed and turned in bed the whole night-tears almost soaking her bedding. She thought her world would come to an end. To her surprise, it dawned again.

Instinctively, Amani switched on her phone. Nuru had tried to call her over twenty times. He had also sent her countless text messages. She blacklisted all his phone numbers, deleted his messages without reading them and blocked him on all social media platforms. Amani then cursed herself for the umpteenth time for falling in love with a Buba man.

She closed her eyes and started humming 'Here Comes the Sun' by The Beatles. Still, Amani felt empty. That's when she remembered her old friend Jacky, a self-proclaimed love doctor. She searched for Jacky's number on her phonebook and dialed it.

"Hello, Jacky. This is Amani."

"Hi, Amani. It's been long since we last talked to each other. I hope you are fine."

"I'm not well, girlfriend," replied Amani

"I thought girls in love are always fine. What's up?"

"He has cheated on me. I'm in pain, dear."

"Hang on for a few minutes. I'm coming to your room." said Jacky.

"I'm waiting for you,"

"Keep on waiting and getting ready, dear. We may take a short walk outside campus."

"Cool," replied Amani before ending the call.

She grabbed her towel and went to the shower room.

Amani bent and turned on the shower faucet. Cold water hit her body. She stood upright, closed her eyes, and faced upward while scrubbing her body with gusto. Amani imagined her past with Nuru being symbolically washed away by water. She twisted her lower lip in disgust at the thought of Nuru. If there was any form of concoction that would help her forget about Nuru, Amani was willing to trade one of her kidneys for it. She spent almost ten minutes in the shower room.

As Amani stepped out of the bathroom, she felt slightly relieved from the heartbreak. She walked to her wardrobe, dropped her towel and grabbed a bottle of lotion. Amani applied it over her whole body. She then applied a taupe eyeshadow, wore flared skirt, a fitted top, black leggings and boots.

Amani admired her image in a full length mirror on the wall of her room. Everything was perfect but her hair was in a mess. She rubbed her head dry using a face towel, applied a light hair serum on it, then picked a comb from her desk and ran it through her hair.

"Hey, Amani," said Jacky as she knocked on the door.

Amani unlocked the door.

"You look beautiful," said Jacky as she embraced her.

"Thank you," replied Amani.

She offered Jacky the only seat in her room before locking the door. Amani sat on the bed.

"Why are you locking the door from inside? He won't behead you."

Amani licked her lips and said, "His sight might choke me to death."

"Excellent! That's a clear indicator you are still in love with him but you are in denial."

"Only in a nightmare," said Amani.

"Amani, you are stressed. As I had suggested earlier, you need to refresh your mind by giving yourself a break from the campus environment. I think visiting an animal orphanage or public park will be a great service to your mental health. Nature is the best remedy to stress," proposed Jacky, eyebrows knitted with concern.

"You were reading my mind, girlfriend. That would definitely be my next plan," said Amani.

"If you're ready, we can visit Nchi Animal Orphanage. It is ten minutes' drive from here."

"Do I look like someone who has just woken up from a rat's hole?" Said Amani as she picked her pouch.

"Good girl. Always ready like a soldier. You only need to be enlightened on matters of love and relationship as you reenergize your mind."

"I've given up on relationships. Men will always lie," said Amani in a spiteful tone.

"Indeed lying is to men while crying is to women."

"I hate all men," Amani retorted while packing a mirror, a packet of wet wipes and a lip-gloss in her pouch.

"The funny thing is that they are like magnets," observed Jacky.

"I've learnt a lesson the hard way; all men are dogs," squawked Amani.

"Did you just say all men are dogs?"

"Oh yes! All men are dogs," Insisted Amani.

"If all men are dogs, then all women are bitches. Amani is a woman, therefore she is a bitch."

"Shut up, Jacky."

"Amani, you must appreciate the fact that men are naturally hunters."

"I see you've been hypnotized by the masculine school of thought."

"History has all the evidence, my sister. It is said that the early human beings were hunters and gatherers. Men were hunters and women were gatherers. Today, modern men are still hunters, not by accident. It's permanently inscribed in their DNA," said Jacky.

"I wonder if men have a heart, leave alone a conscience. Do they cry on a broken relationship? Do they even care that women have a heart and need to be treated and handled with care?"

"For your information, men also cry," said Jacky, swiping her iPhone's screen.

"I completely disagree with you, Jacky. Men have stones for hearts."

Jacky stashed the iPhone in her handbag and said, "You are wrong, girlfriend. Like women, men cry, but they don't cry like women. They cry like fish. They cry from inside."

Amani nodded, not because she agreed to Jacky's arguments, but to conclude the debate.

"After this trip, your mind will be refreshed. I will accompany you to Nuru's room," said Jacky as they stepped out of Amani's room.

"Who is Nuru? That name sounds strange to me," responded Amani, locking her room.

"Are you out of your mind, Amani? Isn't he your boyfriend?"

"Thanks for giving me a clue. Forgive me for being forgetful. I've just recalled. That beast is not my best friend. He is my enemy number one."

"Don't tell me you mean what you say. You've dumped him, just like that?"

"I've not dumped him, he's incapacitated my heart," replied Amani.

"I pity you, girlfriend. I wish you knew."

"Knew what?"

"Buba men are just too hot to be ignored. They are all tall, dark and handsome," said Jacky as she gently patted Amani on the back.

"And above all, unfaithful," retorted Amani.

"But not like the Tetung. I won't ever dare date a Tetung. Those men eat like hungry hyenas, hold onto outdated cultural beliefs and cheat on their wives openly. They believe that a woman must be very submissive to her man. The only good trait that they have is an athletic body."

"What of the Mbayuyus? We used to have a braggart Mbayuyu teacher back in high school. He had a chain of girlfriends. We christened him Mr. Rooster," said Amani.

"Even though Mbayuyu men may have countless girlfriends, they shower all their lovers with generous romance. Amani, if you want to party and party, I recommend you date a Mbayuyu man."

"Mbayuyus sharply contrast with men from my tribe. Hazunda men can do anything including the impossible to get money but rarely spend their hard-earned cash on luxuries."

Jacky laughed and said, "Hazundas are instinctively lovers of money. The only way to differentiate between a dead and a living Hazunda is by tossing a coin. But for your information, never confuse a Hazunda's rags for poverty."

The two ladies sashayed to the taxi stage chatting and laughing girlishly. A sleek Prado pulled to the stage and came to a halt. The side window was lowered slowly revealing a bald- headed man with thick grey beard and moustache.

"What's up ladies? My name is Professor Spencer," he said in a fake Black-American accent.

"Hallo," responded Jacky putting a long stress on the last syllable.

Amani remained quiet. She was too dazed to talk.

"Would you like a ride?" He asked.

"Thank you," responded Jacky in a jovial tone.

She did not wait for further instructions. Jacky got hold of the door and struggled to open it.

"I'm sorry, girl. This door sucks."

He pressed the remote and the door flew open. Jacky sat at the co-driver's seat. Amani was still standing by the posh car, trying to figure out the events unfolding before her.

"Be careful, Jacky," Amani cautioned her friend. "Stop behaving like an elementary kid, Amani." "I believe there's nothing for nothing, Jacky." "You are absolutely right, Amani, but I'm not an anybody. I'm aware that you are students of Taifa University. Dr. Catherine, your Comparative Literature lecturer, is my wife. I work as the permanent secretary in the ministry of state security. Here is my work pass," he said flashing the document then continued, "Get in please, Amani, and make yourself comfortable. You are in safe hands."

Half –heartedly, Amani joined her friend in the car. She occupied the back left seat.

Amani clutched her phone and immersed herself in Facebook. She had two new messages from Derrick. He was beseeching her to talk to Nuru. Amani ignored his messages and blocked him.

Her phone vibrated. She had a new WhatsApp message. She opened it, but to her surprise there was no text, just a love emoji from the Dean of Students.

She raised her head to ensure that neither Jacky nor Prof. Spencer had noted her sudden mood swing. Another surprise embraced Amani, making her to forget about the content of the message she was reading. Jacky's bare thighs were being caressed by Prof Spencer. His right hand was still holding the steering wheel. Prof Spencer released his right hand from the steering wheel, pushed his bushy grey chin towards Jacky's youthful smooth face, and kissed her. Reacting out of feigned pleasure, Amani tilted her head, making the professor surge backwards, hitting the steering wheel. The vehicle swayed out of its lane and raced towards a petroleum tanker, moving at a slow speed. In a moment of seconds, their lives would be no more. Amani screamed. Prof Spencer jumped to the emergency brakes. The vehicle stopped.

"Are you two out of your senses?" Screamed Amani.

"What are you talking about?" hissed Jacky.

"It will be alright, girls. Cool down," said Prof Spencer in a calm tone.

"This woman is envious. She should blame herself for not being pretty enough," Jacky said as she massaged Prof Spencer's shoulders.

"You think I'm ready to sleep with the elder brother of my great grandfather? That's an insult, Jacky."

"Don't you know old cats drink milk too? In fact more stylishly than young ones," said Professor Spencer.

"Tell her," butted in Jacky.

"Don't be fooled by money, Jacky. Get back to your senses."

"Don't be stupid, former Mrs. Nuru?"

"This is unbearable. Stop this car. I want to alight right now," Amani cried.

"Relax!" Screamed Prof Spencer.

"No!" She insisted.

"Just chuck her out of our car. She's a nuisance," Jacky said, throwing her hands in the air.

Prof Spencer stopped the car at a nearby taxi stage. Amani alighted. There were no 'goodbyes.' Professor Spencer drove away immediately. Amani watched the car speeding off until it disappeared from her eyesight.

A tuk-tuk taxi was parked at the stage. She moved close to it and peeped through its window. The taxi had no passenger on board. The driver was chewing *khat*. When he saw Amani, he winked at her.

"Nchi Animal orphanage?" Amani inquired.

"Fifty shillings," replied the driver while shaking his clenched fist.

She boarded the tuk-tuk. Four more passengers joined her.

"I can barely breathe. You've squeezed us in this box like matchsticks," a thick woman seating next to Amani complained.

"If you want a VIP ride, buy your own car," said the driver.

He rolled the key into the ignition. The tuk-tuk roared into action and hit the road, Nchian style. The thick woman slumped against Amani.

"Excuse me, mama. Kindly give me some space," Amani pleaded.

"Who lied to you that I'm your mum?" she said before muttering incomprehensible curses in her native language.

The driver turned left, a few metres past the university senior staff quarters. He overtook other tuk-tuks, to the dissatisfaction of the thick lady.

"Be careful, you are not ferrying sacks of potatoes," she grumbled.

Amani smiled mischievously at her neighbour -turned -foe. She responded by clicking. Amani started humming Leakey Dagger's '*Haters Gonna Choke Themselves to Death.*' A boy suddenly crossed the road. The driver swayed past him, narrowly missing a stationary motorcycle parked at the edge of the road.

"Nchi Animal Orphanage," screamed Amani.

"Alright," said the driver while applying the brakes. Amani handed a fifty shilling coin to him then forced her way past the hefty lady. She fanned her nose using her left hand as Amani's body brushed against her face. Wearing a sarcastic grin, Amani waved at her vigorously-sending all the passengers into laughter.

The main gate to the animal orphanage was locked, an unusual incident on a Saturday morning. There was a long growing queue of tourists snaking up to the tarmac road. Amani abhorred standing in queues. Many choices popped in her mind: walking leisurely back to the university or visiting Taifa Botanical Garden. After weighing her options, she resolved to queue.

Amani stood behind an obese White man, a typical model of a chatterbox. He spoke at the top of his voice, wondering why the international media was committed to feeding the world with predominantly negative images about African countries.

He turned back and faced Amani.

"Hello, when are you planning to open the gate?" He asked.

"Be informed, Black Nchians also travel to public parks using their own money," she said.

"I'm sorry ma'am, I thought you were an employee of the animal orphanage," he apologized.

"Learn to be sensitive," she said.

The man nodded, giving room to silence. Amani on the other hand desired to harangue him the whole day but chose silence. The gate to the animal orphanage was finally opened, revealing a woman in a jungle green blouse and trousers.

"Good morning," she said in a booming voice, "Due to unavoidable circumstances, the park shall remain closed today…"

Tourists booed her. Amani did not wait for her to complete her statement. She adjusted her pouch, slung over her shoulder, and swaggered back to Taifa University.

~ 92 ~

C H A P T E R

13

A cold cloud of mist enveloped Taifa University. The university looked like an open air market, notwithstanding the blood-freezing temperature. The students' union elections would be held the following day. Therefore, campaigns were hitting the apex.

Amani distributed her campaign leaflets at Sankara Garden with renewed energy. The trip to and from the gate of Nchi Animal Orphanage had reenergized her.

"How are you, Amani?" A familiar tenor voice greeted her.

She stopped and looked back. Joseph, one of the most notorious members of Corporal Squad was an inch from her.

"I'm well. How can I help you, Joseph?" Asked Amani.

"Just a second, Amani. I would like to have a word with you aside," said Joseph while rubbing his goatee.

"What is it? Please try to be brief. I have a very tight schedule."

"You know what, Amani?"

"I don't know. Tell me."

"Politics is a game of tricks. A politician with the best tricks wins the day."

"Go straight to the point, Joseph."

"You need to know that your rival in the post for gender affairs secretary general, Jemimah, has already sought our services. She paid us only ten thousand shillings to rig her in. I must admit that I've been secretly supporting you. That's why I'll never be amused to see you losing unfairly," revealed Joseph.

"You people are very honest and kind. Thank you for your genuine concern," said Amani while walking away.

"Wait," he said while following her, "The only favour that I need from you is to pay me fifteen thousand shillings and angels will smile at you. You'll become our new gender affairs secretary without straining much."

"Thank you again my honest friend for being loving and caring," said Amani in a flat monotone while nodding her head.

"You are such a great lady! Get my number, you will send the money to me via mobile money."

Amani turned, held her hips and said, "I will send it to you once I pluck money from a tree growing on my head."

Joseph pointed at her and exclaimed, "Stop mocking me!"

Amani tilted her head then waltzed away while whistling.

Mist slowly melted from the atmosphere as the sun rose. Amani's vision got clearer. In front of her, there was a crowd of students milling around a roadshow truck. Five Toyota Prado cars were parked adjacent to the truck. Members of Corporal Squad surrounded the vehicles. They were wearing blue caps with printed images of Taifa University Students' Union chairperson aspirant, Msonabari.

A scantily dressed female student was sitting on a mega speaker in the trailer. She blew a kiss to the audience. Male students cheered. Psyched, she stood atop the speaker and snapped her fingers. Music wafted from all the four huge speakers in the trailer. She brushed her long Brazilian hair extension backward and twerked like a boneless mermaid.

A male student shot from the crowd and joined her in the trailer. He did ten push-ups then stood beside the dancing lady. The rest of his body was stiff, but his waist shook vigorously. As music reached its climax, he rolled into a backward somersault. He attempted to perform a forward somersault but he slipped and fell off the trailer. His head hit the pavement. The young man groaned then became stiff. The lady continued dancing, unperturbed. Amani clenched her teeth and momentarily closed her eyes in surprise. Two members of Comrades Squad grabbed him from the ground and walked away carrying him towards Taifa University Health Centre.

The music was stopped. A member of Corporal Squad climbed to the trailer. He picked a microphone lying on top of cartoon boxes and puffed on it twice. He then said, "Hello, ladies and gentlemen. I know you know that we are here for the rehearsals. We are getting ready for the victory of the only human who can sneeze while coughing, and the whole world catches a flu. Comrades, put your hands together for honourable Msonabari."

Sound effects of claps boomed from the speakers as Msonabari climbed to the trailer accompanied by four bodyguards.

He was given a microphone. "Comrades power! …It gives me immense pleasure to watch the trailer of tomorrow's celebration. We shall clinch that seat whether they like it or not. I'm aware that we have haters. May they be choked to death by their own venom…Anyway, let me not waste my saliva talking about useless people. You all know that I'm a man of few words and many actions. …In honour of you, tonight I will be holding a big bash in Miriam Makeba Multipurpose Hall. All are welcome. Thank you." He bowed and gave one of his bodyguards the microphone.

Music resumed playing, and the twerking lady jumped back to action. Elated by Msonabari's promise, many students danced and screamed. Amani shook her head and left the scene. That is when she spotted Nuru. He was in a white T- Shirt that was boldly printed, '*SAY YES TO PEACE.*' She immediately changed her way but it was too late. Nuru had already seen her. He waved at Amani as he trotted towards her.

"Keep distance," she screamed. He kept on trotting after her. Amani spit on her left hand and held it high. Nuru stopped, knowing she might slap him. Amani sighed and continued walking.

C H A P T E R

14

𝒯aifa University polling stations were open at 4:30a.m. Members of the Nchi Republic Electoral Commission and external observers had already availed themselves thirty minutes earlier. Amani and her electoral agents too braved the morning cold to ensure that the students' union elections were conducted freely and fairly. As a pre-elections tradition, the electoral commissioners distributed leaflets containing Nchi constitutional laws governing the electoral process to all the contestants and electoral officials present in Tumaini Hall.

Amani read Section (3 i) of the Electoral Act silently, "Any form of bribery, hooliganism, impersonation or any attempt to tamper with the elections results shall lead to automatic disqualification and trial in a criminal court of the concerned person(s) immediately or within a period not exceeding three days after the release of the official elections results." She proceeded to section 3(ii) and read it in a whisper, "Any person(s) found tampering with elections' results or engaging in any form of mannerism as stated in (3i) shall be disqualified by the returning officer in charge while awaiting confirmation or dismissal of charges against him or her in a competent Law court." Energized by section (3ii), she read section 3(iii) aloud, "In the case of 3 (ii), the closest opponent(s) of the aforementioned candidate(s) shall be declared the winner by the returning officer, unless advised otherwise by a competent Law Court."

Nuru and other members of Shiners busied themselves with peace maintenance activities. In a few weeks, the International Peace Forum-Youth Category will be holding its meeting in Taifa University. Should students go on rampage, then Nuru and his allies will suffer a big blow. Amani kept on stealing glances at them. None of her former colleagues seemed to recognize her presence, to her disappointment. Amani's attitude towards Shiners Organization shifted from approval to spiteful. She hated all the activities of Shiners. She hated all its members and supporters. She also hated herself for failing to understand why she hated an organization that she once loved and participated in all its activities.

At noon, the sun's heat had tripled; robbing electorates of their comfort but sparing their determination to vote. Students held umbrellas above their heads. A strong wave of laughter suddenly swept through the long queues, shaking everyone to the core. Jonah, the university clown famously known as Big Baby, was the source of the wave. He was walking towards the crowd, swinging his waist girlishly and talking to invisible friends. It was rumoured in Taifa University that when he was not under the influence of marijuana or illicit brew, he took no chance in cracking jokes that were worth the title jokes. In a special response to the electorates' applause, he thumped his feet on the ground, went down on his knees, faced the unpromising sky and sung in a guttural voice, "My dearest rain, come. Coome. Cooome." He stopped after realizing that everybody, including the security officers were laughing at him. Once the laughter subdued, he screamed in a shrill voice, "Rain, come." He took in a very long breath and yelled, "Pardon me for the pun". The electorates broke into a louder laughter. Jonah sprang on his toes, stretched his neck forward, frowned then took off very fast.

Trouble started after Jonah's departure. A male student was frog-marched out of the voting hall.

"You won't prevent me from exercising my constitutional rights," he screamed

"Not at the expense of the rights of other students. You can't vote twice. It's wrong," said a security officer.

"Stop poking an intellect," bellowed the student.

The security officer grabbed the culprit's head and knocked it against a concrete pillar.

"Leave me alone. I am innocent," he cried.

The tussle attracted the attention of the returning officer.

"Young man, you are committing a crime on top of a crime. Thank your lucky stars. Were it not for my fatherly concern, right now you'd be resting in a police cell. Now, if your wits serve you correctly, disappear from our vicinity."

He turned to the electorates and said, "My sons and daughters, let's maintain law and order. I know you are aware that one of your colleagues invented a device that helps in reducing electoral irregularities. Please be on the lookout."

The rotten matter of Taifa University continued to present its ugly head as time advanced. A high-pitched scream emerged from the entrance to the voting hall. A female student was receiving a rain of lashes on her back. The security officer was holding her by the collar bone as she struggled to be released. The young lady's handbag and T-shirt were torn. She removed a pair of tweezers from her torn handbag and squeezed it into the security officer's abdomen. He groaned and freed her. She fled the scene like a 100 m race competitor in an Olympics championship. Her wig fell off her head but she did not stop to pick it.

"See, she was having a dozen ballot papers", said the security officer while ruffling the papers. He entered the voting hall with the papers.

Nchi electoral commissioners continued to tally votes in Tumaini Hall. Students were invited in the hall to witness the votes counting exercise. Large screens erected in strategic places updated the public after every three minutes about the elections results.

The provisional results indicated that Leornard Lindi was leading in the position of chairperson, followed very closely by Msonabari. In position three was Stanley Lolo. There was less competition in the seat that Amani was eyeing. Her opponent had 2050 votes while she followed with 42 votes.

Five hours later, the returning officer announced the final results, "Ladies and gentlemen, I would like to congratulate most of you for voting peacefully in the concluded Taifa University Students Union elections. The results indicate that in the post for secretary general, Jamal

Adan is the winner with 2300 votes against Aimable Bosco who garnered 2203 votes." Mbayuyu and Tetung students went frenzy in celebration. "Hey! Calm down. In the seat of gender affairs secretary, Jedidah Tendo is the winner with 4039 votes against Amani Salo's 101 votes."

Everyone laughed at Amani. She remained alert, unmoved by the results.

"Silence, please. I may take disciplinary action against you for gross misconduct... In the Chairperson's position, Msonabari has won with 8027 votes. The first runner is..."

Ululations and screams filled the hall. Students from Hazunda, Gebo and a few minor tribes burst into celebration. They grabbed Msonabari and lifted him shoulder high.

"We've won. The seat is ours. Thanks be to God," they chanted as they marched out of the hall. They danced along the pavements and corridors of Taifa University while holding each other's arms in solidarity.

"Unity is strength," they sung.

Deafening songs and chants made by pro-Msonabari students graduated to pandemonium. Bottles of beer were cracked and obscenities uttered. As if acting from a cue, anti-Msonabari students from Corporal Squad ganged up swiftly and charged towards the celebrating multitude. The two groups drew towards each other. Insults that appealed to tribal stereotypes were exchanged.

A member of an anti-Msonabari group pelted a bottle of whiskey filled with dirty water. It flew in the air like a propelled rocket, spraying its content in all directions. The bottle landed in the middle of the pro-Msonabari crowd. Nobody was hit or hurt. It fell on the pavement breaking into small pieces of glasses, scattering the crowd.

"Msonabari is Taifa University's chairperson. Haters, go hug a transformer," A student screamed.

"We can't allow. Msonabari was rigged in," an anti-Msonabari student yelled.

Part of the two antagonistic groups started to engage each other in a physical tussle. Others moved to the lecture halls, library, hostels, cafeteria, students' centre and swimming pool to fight their enemies. Wasn't the war on, Mbayuyu – Tetung combined vs Gebo-Hazunda combined?

Garang Lecture Hall had turned into a battlefield of emotions. Hazunda and Gebo students- major supporters of Msonabari- sat on one side of the hall; away from their opponents, the Mbayuyu and Tetung. A huge space was created in the middle of the hall. Between the two rival tribal blocs, sat Nuru; alone but not lonely.

Dr. Watson Brown, lecturer of East African Literature, stood in front of his students, hands akimbo. The Briton literary academician was a strong critic of Nchi's politics. He bared his murky teeth, twirled his overgrown beards then adjusted the suspenders that made him to appear like a marionette. Smiling wryly at his students, Dr. Watson walked with a mocking limp to the centre of the lecture hall, outstretched his arms (each facing the two antagonistic groups), and clapped them. The class was silent. No murmur. No jeer.

"A very good morning to you, ladies and gentlemen. Today we are going to have an overview of the thematic concerns of the first generation of East African poets and novelists. The likes of Okot p' Bitek, Ngugi wa Thiong'o, Micere wa Mugo, Timothy Wangusa among others. To kick-start our lecture today, I ask, what are some of the thematic concerns in the works of the first generation of East African literary writers?"

Both sides had many hands in the air, an unusual incident in Taifa University.

"Politics."

"No, it ought to be dirty politics."

"Corruption."

"Theme of unity," said Nuru stressing every syllable. Students from both sides stared at him in awe.

"There is also another major theme that none of you has mentioned. The theme of alienation that was as a result of the then primitive African society failing to fully embrace modernity introduced to them by White settlers and missionaries," said Dr. Watson putting emphasis on 'then primitive African' and 'White.'

Nuru raised his hand and challenged the lecturer's argument, "I beg to differ with you, Dr. Watson. As far as civilization is concerned, no society has ever and will never be primitive. That's the problem with Westerners. Sorry, I mean a few people with an imperialist mentality. A culture that is different from the so called first world countries is automatically termed primitive and barbaric."

"A point of correction, sir," shouted Dorcas from the Tetung-Mbayuyu tribal bloc, "Alienation is when one lacks identity. Alienation is when one abandons his kinsmen, tribe and culture then behaves like an empty entity in space. On top of that, an alienated person according to existentialists' poetics is a lone individual amidst a crowd, undergoing intense suffering and has a sense of lack of belonging. With that, I rest my case."

"Dorcas has pointed out a very critical point. Nuru, do you have any contribution to challenge or support Dorcas' deduction?" Inquired the lecturer with finality.

"Thank you, Dr. Watson. Literature exists in time and space. Therefore, any example given in literature, just like in real life, must be contextualized. Failure to do so brings out a misleading interpretation or unscholarly arguments that are emotionally driven. Allow me to use Okot p`Bitek's book, 'Song of Lawino.' What happens to Ocol in 'Song of Lawino?' He is alienated from his culture. Isn't he? What causes his alienation? Isn't it a foreign culture imposed on him? Colonization brought alienation in Nchi and alienation brought divisions. Look at the sitting arrangement in this lecture hall. You may call it what you'd like but I call it the bitter fruit of colonization."

Dr. Watson interrupted, "I politely disagree with you, Nuru. You ought to know that Africans have been known to highly value their tribes and clans since time immemorial."

Nuru raised his hand, ready to counter the lecturer's argument, but he was ignored.

"We will not waste time on alienation. There are other themes that need to be discussed. Let's start with violence, an aspect that has been paralyzing poor Africa." A student from the Gebo-Hazunda tribal bloc raised his hand and said, "According to the Fanonian philosophy that found its way in the works of a few first-generation East African literary writers, there are two types of violence: brutal and redemptive violence. In 'A Grain of Wheat' by Ngugi wa Thiong'o, we see the cure to the colonialists' brutal violence is redemptive violence, executed by African freedom fighters. I therefore disagree with you, Dr. Watson, when you say violence is completely bad. We ought to examine both sides of the coin."

Nuru chipped in, "In that context, I think Africans' way of acting violently was clearly justified but I disagree when violence is enforced to justify a selfish…."

"No! We can't allow," roared an anti-Msonabari group of students as they burst into the lecture hall. Dr. Watson was kicked out of the hall. Students too were not spared- they were forced to join the protesters. Those who attempted to resist were whipped. Nuru neither talked nor walked. He sat on the floor of the lecture hall as dozens of strokes descended on him.

"Shame on you!" A pro-Msonabari group stomped the hall, distracting Nuru's tormentors. Screams filled the air and blood spilled everywhere. Within seconds, it became an I-kill-you-or-you-kill-me affair.

A police jeep came to a screeching halt at the parking lot of the administration block. Two officers jumped out of the vehicle. In Nchi republic, police officers and university students were like like poles of different magnets. It is for this reason that warring students stopped the fight and scampered in all directions. Calm returned on campus.

C H A P T E R

15

$\mathcal{A}$mani felt miserable. Things that mattered to her had turned to wreckage. From a broken relationship to an embarrassing defeat in the students' union elections. In a university where money speaks louder than manifestos, Amani knew from the beginning of her campaigns that her victory would be like selling woolen sweaters in the middle of the Kalahari Desert. However, she had not prepared herself psychologically to handle loss. Her defeat sent her from frustration to depression. For the past ten days, she spent most of her time indoors- cursing, reading and writing poems. In her moment of self-isolation, Amani had written thirteen poems. Reading her own poems gave her a glimmer of hope.

Unfortunately, another mishap smacked Amani unannounced. She could not locate her poems in her laptop. Amani clicked on the recycle bin, but there was nothing apart from ambiguous programs.

"My precious poems are lost!" She cried.

A knock was heard on her door.

Submerged in a sad mood, Amani was hesitant to respond. However, the knock was persistent and urgent.

"Please come in," she said to save herself from the noise.

Nuru swaggered into her room accompanied by Julius.

"What do you want in my room?" Screamed Amani.

"Amani, I told you we've haters, you didn't believe."

"I'm sorry, Nuru. I'm very sorry, Amani. It was my fault. I regret," chipped in Julius.

Amani rose from her bed and moved close to the two men.

"What is wrong with you, men? So, you think all women are gullible?"

"Amani, I swear, nobody is playing games on you," said Nuru.

She silenced him and screamed, "Get out of my room right now."

"Kindly give us audience. Just a minute," pleaded Nuru.

Amani did not respond. She folded her arms in front of her chest and pounced on them with her eyes. Nuru defended himself by stoning her with the truth, "Julius is the cause of our split. He's the one who sent me that love message." Amani's eyes did not blink. Nuru panted. Overpowered by the impact of Amani's eyes and Nuru's words, Julius fell prostate between the ex-lovers and spit out mountains of apologies. Amani laughed at him. Nuru moved closer to her. She retreated and gave him a sweeping contemptuous look from head to shoes.

"The naked truth lies in Julius' phone and mine. They say seeing is believing. Here you are," said Nuru as he handed the two phones to her. She took the phones from him and dumped them in a dustbin.

"That's very unreasonable, Amani," said Nuru.

"So was your childish skit. It is my turn to entertain you, men. Keep on waiting."

She bent over her sink and pulled a bucket full of water. Amani lifted the bucket with both hands, ready to pour its content on her ex-boyfriend. Nuru did not move. He stood still, eyes fixed on her. A sharp pain coiled in her head. The bucket slipped from her hands; spilling water on the floor. Julius- clothes partially soaked-shot up from the floor.

"Go ahead, Amani. Pour water on me. Pour water on me for speaking the truth. Pour water on me for proving to you my innocence. Pour water on me now. Please be quick," said Nuru as tears threatened to burst out of his eyes.

"I regret my actions. Please forgive me, friends," mumbled Julius.

Amani tried to speak, but strong emotions failed her. She broke into tears.

"I think you need sufficient time alone before making a sound conclusion. I will be waiting for you in my room in case you need to talk to me."

Nuru pushed Julius from his way and walked out of Amani's room. Julius ran after him, muttering a thousand and one apologies.

Amani remained immobile, sobbing spiritedly as if it had been declared world sobbing day. Her lips dried, neck stiffened and muscles weakened. Amani became aware of the self-destruction deeds she was committing. For that reason, she shut her mouth, closed her eyes and drained her mind of negative thoughts. The headache subsided but her muscles weakened further.

Burning with curiosity, Amani attempted to move towards the dustbin, but her frail muscles failed her. She trembled clumsily in one position-teeth chattering. It took Amani several tries to move her feet forward. Gently, she lowered her right hand into the waste bin and got hold of the two android phones. A thin film of dust had covered their screens. Amani wiped them clean with the hem of her t-shirt. She swiped the screen of Nuru's phone. It was unlocked.

Just as Amani was about to tap on 'messages,' cool rushing air slapped her on the face. She lifted her chin, raised her eyebrows and faced the door to her room. It had been flung open. Nancy and Derrick were standing there. Shocked, Amani unfurled a cosmetic smile to cover her troubled frame. She feared; a rattling cry might part her lips and complicate that awkward moment. Nancy stumbled on her high heels before getting hold of Amani.

"You are seriously unwell," whispered Nancy as she sat her on bed.

Amani gasped. Nancy studied her.

"Who has hurt you?" Derrick asked.

Amani's gut somersaulted painfully at that query. A strong urge to cry rose in her oesophagus. She held her throat, sank deeper in bed and shook her head

"Let's rush her to the health centre," suggested Nancy.

Amani wondered why she was allowing herself to react like a fragile brat. She forced herself to laugh at herself. Nancy and Derrick joined her in the laughing ceremony though unaware of the cause of her laughter.

"You guys are convinced that I'm unwell. I was just acting. I am very fine."

"Never joke with a Literature student. She can laugh all the way through pain," commented Derrick.

"And never joke with a Computer Science student. He can hack into your mind, download your thoughts and tell you your real character," added Nancy as she winked at Derrick.

"Leave me alone," snapped Amani.

"We won't leave you alone, girlfriend. Where is Nuru?" Asked Nancy.

The dead pain in her head resurrected. She swallowed a huge lump of saliva and maintained silence; fighting the urge to cry.

"Never joke with a Journalism student. She can reveal your real emotion with her probing question," remarked Derrick with the hope of making Amani to open up.

"You make me angry. Stop it please."

"We won't stop it, unless we see you laughing sincerely. Now give me these phones," said Nancy while snatching Julius' phone from Amani's hand.

"What is disturbing you, Amani? Is it love?" asked Nancy.

"Love? Why?"

"You know better than me."

"I don't know what you are talking about, Nancy."

"I know you know what I'm talking about. It's written on your face. It's written on the lips of everyone on campus."

"Everyone knows?"

"Is that a confession?"

"No, I just didn't know love can turn tragic. Now the joke is on me," cried Amani.

"Tragic? Wrong diction. To love is to accept the two faces of love unconditionally: pleasure and pain," said Nancy.

"I feel betrayed."

"Ask yours truly to write about her love life and ten romance novels will be produced. Ask a Literature professor to analyze those books, and she will point out betrayal as one of the major themes. By the way, what do you mean by 'I feel betrayed?'"

With great effort, Amani opened her heart. She spoke about her past love life with Nuru; Julius' attempt to make her believe Nuru was cheating on her with Beryl; the love message that popped into Nuru's phone when they were soaring high in romance and her swift decision to end their relationship.

Amani felt naked after exposing the cause of her breakup with Nuru. She stopped speaking, ushering a short silence in the room. Nancy used that time to scrutinize the phone in her right hand.

"Why are you using Julius' photo as a screen saver?" Asked Nancy.

Amani hesitated. Unable to hide anything anymore, she spoke about her latest interaction with Julius and Nuru.

"So, this phone belongs to Julius?" Inquired Nancy.

Amani nodded.

"Fine. We're good to go. Check the inbox of Nuru's phone and I will browse through Julius' 'sent' folder," suggested Nancy.

After two minutes of scrutinizing dozens of messages, Amani screamed, "Here is the damn message."

"Dated?" Asked Nancy, still fumbling with Julius' phone.

"25th March."

"Read it, please," requested Nancy.

"No, do your homework. I'm dying to find the truth."

"There are so many love messages sent to various recipients," complained Nancy.

"It starts with '*Hi honey.*'"

Nancy took a few seconds before responding, "I've found it."

Amani dropped Nuru's phone on the bed and grabbed Julius' phone from Nancy. Nancy squealed, right hand clutching air. Amani twisted her lips, held Julius' phone with both hands and started reading the love message.

As she read the love message, Amani felt a strong therapeutic energy slithering through her nerves and raiding every cell in her body. Her body muscles loosened. Nonetheless, she kept on reading and re-reading the love message. As Amani kept on re-reading the love message, her loose muscles got colonized by loneliness. Loneliness whose cure was only known to her heart.

"Do you still need my service?" Asked Derrick.

Amani shook her head and said, "I'm ashamed of myself. The truth has dawned on me. I was blinded by emotions. Poor me, where will I hide my face?"

"Cool down. Nigerians say, no matter how big a nose is, it can neither smell nor see danger. Shit happened to you, it happens and it will happen. Though hurt, I'm glad you've learnt from your past," said Nancy.

Amani responded by granting her a big grin.

"That's a genuine grin," observed Derrick.

"Thank you, friends, for your support."

"You're always welcome, Amani. By the way, I bet you have no idea why Derrick and I are here. Well, I gave you a USB flash drive to copy spoken word clips from it. Didn't I?"

"Yes, you did, but it's corrupted. I have lost all my poems."

"Don't worry. That's why we are here. I erroneously transferred that virus to Nancy's netbook while installing a recovery software in her machine," said Derrick.

Nancy interjected, "And I, with my inexcusable ignorance, copied infected files from my laptop to my flash disk. I've just learnt this morning that all my files have been corrupted. Thinking that my flash disk was the source of the virus; I called you but you did not receive my call. I called Derrick later, and here we are."

"Where did Derrick get the virus?"

"As you know, I've developed a computer program that helps in curbing electoral frauds. It is truly unique. However, not everyone is pleased with my accomplishment. Few of my friends have unsuccessfully tried to hack into my laptop. Others have been sending me email attachments with spy programs and viruses. In short, that's how I got 'Friend' the virus."

"I swear genuine friends are becoming endangered species," exclaimed Amani.

"Excuse me, guys, but I must leave now. I have to attend a lecture on Broadcast Media Production," said Nancy.

"I have to leave too. Later in the afternoon, I will clean your laptop, install for you an anti-virus software and recover all your lost files."

Amani ululated and hugged Derrick.

"In future, learn to scan any external storage device for viruses every time you insert it in your laptop," said Derrick as he freed himself from her.

Ten seconds in the lift felt like eternity. Amani disembarked on the sixth floor of Kilimanjaro Hostel and made for her ex-boyfriend's room.

Julius was sitting on the thresh-old of Nuru's room, face buried between his own thighs. Amani's footsteps attracted his attention. He sat upright, threw his eyes on her and followed her movements. Every movement of her feet stabbed his conscience with guilt.

"I'm sorry," he muttered as he rose.

She disregarded him, strutted straight to Nuru's door and pounded on it repeatedly.

"He won't open it. He thinks I'm the one knocking. Call out his name," said Julius.

"Nuru," shouted Amani while hitting the door with all her strength.

"Give me a second," screamed Nuru from inside.

Amani became calm. She could hear some movements inside the room. Click! The door was opened. The two ex-lovers faced each other again. Nuru did not trust his eyes. He froze on the floor. Amani took a step forward, then another and flew into his arms. Nuru took charge; he embraced her so tightly that they could hardly breathe.

"Have you forgiven me, Nuru?" She inquired while quivering.

Nuru lowered his head, closed his eyes and kissed her.

"I love you, my gentle one. It was not your fault."

She pressed her head on her boyfriend's chest and then thrust it left and right to wipe away the overflowing tears from her eyes. All the while, Nuru stroke her back gently.

"I 'm sorry for what I did to you two?" Said Julius as he entered the room.

"What made you to betray your friend, Mr. Judas Iscariot?" Yelled Amani. There was silence. "I'm speaking to you." She tried to dive at him but Nuru restrained her.

"The devil misled me," he croaked like a sick frog.

"Which devil?" screamed Nuru.

"I was jealous of you two. I felt you were rising to fame rather too fast than I expected. From the bottom of my heart, accept my utmost apologies."

Nobody responded. Shamefacedly, Julius went down on his knees, crawled to the duo and cried on their feet, "I'm very sorry. Forgive me, please."

Amani bent down and held his right hand. Nuru followed suit. He held his left hand.

"Please stand up. I've forgiven you," Amani said in a whisper.

"I've forgiven you, Julius," mumbled Nuru.

Julius rose up, bowed before the love birds and said, "Thank you."

"You may leave at your own pleasure," said Amani.

"It's not over yet. I'm afraid."

"What is it again?" asked Nuru.

"I'm still being haunted by guilt. I would like to have peace of mind. Please promise me that you won't take any legal action against me after revealing to you a secret."

"If we've pardoned you for breaking us apart, then what will bar us from forgiving you for any misdeed that you did to us in the past?" Jabbered Nuru.

"My roommate, Jerry, is one of the gang leaders of Corporal Squad. Most of their meetings were held in my room and I'm ashamed to admit that I frequently took part in their discussions. I once directed them to your room but they mistakenly broke into your neighbour's room and injured him. I was being used by Corporal Squad to bring you down. I implore you, Nuru and Amani, forgive me."

"I've forgiven you," said Nuru without straining.

C H A P T E R

16

"*P*hew! No more students' elections," said Amani while clutching Nuru's right hand.

Nuru squeezed her palm as they walked down the stairs of Kilimanjaro Hostel. The number of students on campus had reduced drastically, thanks to the forthcoming Nchi general elections and Taifa University long holiday. The postponement of the end-of-semester examinations as recommended by the newly-elected Taifa University Students' Union Council had worsened the situation. Exams were the only factor that bound most students to campus.

"It feels super-good to have you back, my queen," said Nuru, breaking the silence.

Amani closed her eyes and said, "Awww! Don't mention it. I will cry."

"What if I remind you that you are a Black beauty with brains? Will you still cry, my queen?" asked Nuru, locking his eyes on Amani.

She blushed. He kissed her forehead. A handful of students walked past them, pulling suitcases.

"Let's sit there," he said, pointing at a concrete bench by the pavement.

As they sat, Nuru took off his brown leather jacket and placed it on his laps.

"By the way, have you realized everyone is in a hurry to vacate the university?" Asked Amani.

"We also need to leave very soon. The general elections will be held next week."

"I hope national elections are different from what I experienced here. I gave up on campus politics. It drove me to depression," said Amani.

"I'm sure your unmatched determination will take you places. You have a bright future in national politics."

Amani giggled.

"I even wrote a special poem for you after elections results were announced," whispered Nuru.

"When did you learn to flatter me?" Asked Amani, smiling.

"I sent it to you through WhatsApp, but you had blocked me."

He pulled his phone and swiped its screen.

"I'm resending it right now."

Amani's phone buzzed instantly.

"Read it for me. Your deep voice has a pleasant way of hypnotizing me," said Amani while leaning forward.

"Thanks. Your request is my command. The poem is titled '*Your Dream.*'

Dear Amani,
Dreams don't die

They live in us forever
Everyone has a dream
A dream to educate
A dream to emancipate
A dream to write
A dream to unite
Like a lioness running after an antelope
Pursue your dream in zest
Never retreat
Never surrender
Never get discouraged
Eye on your dream"

"Wow! That's a beautiful piece of art," remarked Amani.

"You've got a perfect prince charming. I envy you," said Nuru.

The two burst into laughter. Nuru's phone vibrated, cutting short their laughter. Amani shifted uneasily on the bench. An unexpected text message had separated them temporarily. She tried to keep her eyes off the screen of his phone but they darted back involuntarily. It was Derrick calling.

"Hi, Derrick. What's up, buddy?"

"Hi, Nuru. Where are you?"

"We're still on campus," replied Nuru.

"I'm in town. I've borrowed my dad's car. I'll be there after twenty minutes. If you don't mind, I will offer you guys a lift to Feriani City Country Bus Terminus."

"We'll be waiting for you. Thanks, bro," said Nuru before Derrick ended the call.

"Derrick has promised to give us a lift to town."

"What a pleasant coincidence!" Said Amani

"We're lucky to have good friends. They are the reason why we the Shiners will be hosting the whole world after the general elections."

"Why should the international meeting be scheduled shortly after Nchi's general elections?"

"We better get ready very fast, dear. Our buddy should not be kept waiting," said Nuru, avoiding to respond to Amani's question.

She shook her head, unsatisfied with his response. To evade more critical questions, he rose and helped her to stand.

"Think about the question that I asked you," said Amani.

He nodded and held her hand. They walked side by side to her room in Wangare Maathai Hostel.

C H A P T E R

17

*T*hree weeks at home felt like a day in paradise. Amani prayed that the long holiday would be prolonged. Eating, sleeping and reading never bored her. Amani was so submerged in comfort that she was unable to differentiate days of the week. However, Monday the 6th could not creep away from her unnoticed.

Nchi general elections would be held on that day and she was eager to vote for the first time in a general election. Amani had caught a glimpse of Nchi's past chaotic elections marred with irregularities and violence. She was a minor then and hardly knew anything about democracy and mature politics. The more time elapsed, the more impatient she became. Amani wished she had wings to fly from their backyard to the polling station.

Her grandmother, dressed in a multi-coloured *Kitenge* dress, walked to the backyard. She was not the same woman Amani used to know six years ago- old, sickly and bedridden. Amani's grandmother looked sixteen years younger.

Mrs. Salo had received constant sharp criticism from her relatives for neglecting her poor mother. On the other hand, the womenfolk of Tibo did what they were best known for; gossiping. Their sharp diction dug her. However, she used to maintain that she was too poor to cater for her ailing mother's needs, notwithstanding her gigantic financial muscles. Words too can dig as deep as a sword, so they say. Mrs. Salo felt the criticisms were unbearable and ultimately took in her mother.

Amani vacated her seat and sat on the concrete floor.

"Have a seat, grandma."

"Thank you, my co-wife".

A pet German Shepherd dog belonging to Amani's younger brother, Junior, rubbed itself against their feet then barked. Slightly angered, Amani kicked it away.

"How are your studies, my co-wife?"

"Everything is fine, grandma."

"Are you sure?"

"Yes, granny."

"What about your relationship with other students, are you on good terms?" She asked while studying Amani's eyes. Amani was struck by surprise like lightning. She remained silent for a while, licked her dry lips and stared at the thin layers of barren clouds scattered above her head. After a long struggle with her conscience, she said, "Everything is perfect."

"Are you sure?"

"Very sure," she whispered.

The old woman grabbed her granddaughter's left hand, stared at it then muttered something in an unknown language under her breath.

"Look at me directly in the eyes, my co-wife. I am the one talking to you, not the sky," she said, tilting Amani's head.

She continued, "Judging from your mother's dream and your physical appearance, I smell trouble in you. Something is wrong."

"What was the dream all about, granny?"

"I won't tell you unless you confirm what I'm saying. Is it true that your soul is not at peace?"

"Absolutely, but I'm not ready to tell you what is troubling me. Please give me time."

"Peace be with you, daughter of my daughter. Two days ago, my daughter who is your mother, had a strange dream. She was standing alone in total darkness on an anonymous land. Suddenly, her left hand and leg begun to produce light."

"Then what happened?"

"As her limbs continued to glow, men and women in a wide range of clothes with mixed diverse accents and different skin complexions walked, danced and sang in a sweet harmonious voice, basking in the light shining from her limbs. Accidentally, your mother uttered an offensive word against a man singing in an accent synonymous with a tribe that our people look down upon. In a blink of an eye, the jovial crowd vanished. Her limbs, too, ceased to emit light. Engulfed in darkness; your mother became stranded and was unable to move."

"What could be the meaning of that dream?"

"My co-wife, you are a rising star."

"What do you mean?"

"The left hand and leg are feminine limbs as far as our cultural beliefs are concerned. Apart from that, when a woman's left hand glows in any dream, her daughter will be married to a very rich chief. For your case, I can see your star rising beyond the sky, beyond our tribe, beyond ordinary boundaries. I can see your star bringing light to people indiscriminatingly." She stopped talking abruptly, looked left and right to ensure that nobody was eavesdropping at their conversation, then got closer to Amani. "I must tell you my co-wife, all is not well. You have hurdles. Your mother is the biggest obstacle."

"Granny, you are wise."

"I 'm glad your mother's condescending attitude towards our traditions hasn't influenced you."

"Yours truly is a proud African. If I don't like me, who will? The trees?"

"Now I understand why sometimes priestesses bear thieves and witches bear priestesses. I am not surprised."

"You've lost me there."

"My daughter is trapped in an African body. Anything related to Africanism is barbaric. According to her and people of her type, the White man's culture is the ideal."

Amani unzipped her hand bag, removed her lip gloss and mirror. She dabbed her lips with the jelly as she admired her image on the mirror.

"Daughter of my daughter, you are very noble and need to be connected with our ancestors."

"How possible is that?"

"That's why I am called grandmother, a mother of generations. Be silent and you'll listen."

She pulled out of her ankle one of her nine bangles woven with red and white beads then held it above her head. She faced Mt. Tonge and uttered, "May the spirits of our great ancestors join you, Amani Salo, noble daughter of my daughter in your endeavours and struggles."

She uttered the names of heroes of their clan then slid the bangle onto Amani's left arm. Amani stared at the bangle in admiration.

"Our people are dependent on rainfall and sunshine for survival. Red stands for the sun and white stands for rain. I have given you sunshine and rain, noble daughter of my daughter."

Amani's brother, Junior, came running towards them from the house.

"When shall you go with me to Feriani city?" He asked Amani.

"Tomorrow."

"Why is granny's face ugly?"

"Shut up, Junior! Who taught this child ill manners?" Amani said as she pinched him.

"Leave him alone, daughter of my daughter. It is normal at that age."

"Hey, everybody! Come on. I'm ready," shouted Mrs. Salo outside the garage while brandishing her car keys. Amani walked slowly beside her grandmother while Junior trailed behind them, shooting questions at them.

Mrs. Salo drove her car out of the compound. She had learnt to drive gently two years ago after ramming into a caterpillar while over speeding to work. "Mum, my teacher asked me the name of my father. What is it?" Junior asked the innocent but haunting question.

"He is God," Mrs. Salo answered him while praying silently that he would not trouble her further.

"God? Why hasn't He visited us?"

"Junior, stop disturbing mum. She is tired," butted in Amani.

"Mum is not your mum. I'll beat you."

"You are my brother. Your mum is my mum and never speak disrespectfully to anyone. That's bad manners. Violence is also unacceptable. Do you hear me, Junior?" Asked Amani.

Junior nodded.

"You need to learn good manners, my grandson"

"Yes, granny," replied Junior.

."Story, story."

"Story come, granny," said Junior'

"Once upon a time, when the world was still young…."

"Go ahead, granny. I hope the story has songs and monsters."

She narrated the story to her grandson with the art of a good storyteller. Occasionally, Junior would interrupt by asking questions or sing along his grandmother in the chorus of songs that punctuated the oral narrative.

Mrs. Salo drove to the polling station. Through the tinted windows of the vehicle, Amani saw long queues. Police officers moved up and down to ensure everything was in order. Their vehicle's buzz attracted the electorates' attention. Many faces glowed with cosmetic smiles- reserved for welcoming politicians. Amani's mother parked her car at the parking lot alongside eight others. She asked Junior to remain in the vehicle.

The three ladies alighted from the car. Their appearance melted the euphoria of the electorates who were in dire need of a politician. A good politician who would lubricate their hands with something small. What of the hawk-eyed officers maintaining law and order? Were they not part of the human species that occasionally became chaotic to be orderly? Wouldn't wads of new bank notes do magic in rendering them docile?

The crowd speculated in hushed voices: *"You see that Hazunda woman. She killed her husband in order for her to devour assets that they had struggled to accumulate together for more than a decade. Her in-laws swore to avenge on the death of their brother. That's why she fled to this part of the country."*

"You are lying. She is a corporate commercial sex worker. She sells her body to old White men. Haven't you been seeing enough of them flooding her house?"

"She is a devil worshipper. She sacrificed her husband to one of their gods in order for her to become richer."

A few of Mrs. Salo's staff mates were part of the crowd. She greeted them and exchanged jokes with them amid laughter. One of the officers on duty became infuriated by their loud laughter. "Shut up! This is not a hair salon," he said with a rattling voice, his pale yellow eyes fixed on the ladies, waiting for a single word that would provoke him to flex his muscles on them. Mrs. Salo and her friends were not aliens in Nchi. They were familiar with the beastly nature of police officers in their country, thus they held their tongues.

"Hi auntie, you look cool," remarked a male teenager donning a tight-fitting pair of black jeans trousers, Liverpool jersey and a pair of cheap sun glasses, which rested on his forehead. He forced his way into the queue in front of Amani. "Thank you," Amani replied with a cold smile.

"My utmost apologies," said the young man.

"No ill feeling harboured, dude."

"By the way who are you voting for?" He asked in a whisper.

"Sorry, man. Even my nose is not aware," replied Amani

"I advise you to vote for Dr. Manoja in the presidential seat, Mato for the member of parliament post and the youthful Felistus in the gubernatorial position," he said in Nchi's urban lingua, unconscious of the Gonda accent that punctuated his speech. The three politicians he was referring to were from Gonda ethnic group.

"Bernard high! The cock of Nchi high!" Shouted a drunkard brandishing a portrait of Mr. Bernard Kanemu, aspiring governor for Tibo County. A pair of police officers knocked him to the ground, whipped and kicked him repeatedly. His white shirt got soaked in his own blood, but it was an insufficient reason to stop them from giving him a thorough beating.

"That's unconstitutional," a middle- aged woman cried. A heavy slap on her cheek was enough to silence her.

The poor man was handcuffed and thrown into an awaiting land rover like a sack of carrots. Another man could be heard screaming in the voting hall.

"Please forgive me," he implored.

"Why did you double register?" An authoritative voice cut him short.

Lashes of leather whips accompanied him to the land rover. For a moment, Amani stared at her grandmother who was in front of her. The old woman was composed and unmoved. She turned back and faced her mother who was also in a relaxed mood.

C H A P T E R

18

$\mathcal{A}$mani remained glued to her phone at the back seat of the car, watching the live news coverage of the votes counting exercise via YouTube. It was a slow but perfect activity conducted by electoral experts under keen surveillance of international observers, and members of the media. That was not the Nchi whose image had been tarnished by past post-elections violence and electoral irregularities. Nchi was perennially listed among the top five saddest and hopeless countries in the world.

"When are you travelling back to campus for the International Peace Conference?" Her mother asked.

"In the course of next week," replied Amani.

"Why the hurry, my girl?"

"Top officials of International Peace Conference scheduled the AGM to take place immediately after our general elections. Mischievous creatures! They thought Nchi would plunge into post-elections violence so that they may have a reason to find a non-African host nation. Nchi is

129

peaceful and we must host the International Peace Forum's AGM next week. "

""I like the direction which your group is taking. You said it is called Shiners. Right?" said Mrs. Salo.

"Exactly. Our charismatic and organized chairperson has played a pivotal role in shaping Shiners Organization. I love him. Sorry, we love him," replied Amani.

Mrs Salo laughed and said, "You must be in love with him, but why haven't you introduced him to me? I can't wait to have such a visionary son-in-law."

"Surprise. He is the Buba young man whom you insulted on phone."

"Stop messing up with my mood," retorted Mrs. Salo as she lowered the volume of the MP3 player.

Amani shifted her eyes to the congested streets of Tibo town. New modern structures undergoing construction dotted the town. In three years' time, Tibo will have changed for the better, Amani thought as she redirected her attention to her phone. She exited the Nchi National TV Channel on YouTube and browsed international online dailies. Their headlines were screaming and bleeding: *Boko Haram Militiamen Bomb a Church in Northern Nigeria... Another Chinese Writer Jailed... The U.S Named World's Number One Hub of Child Pornography... Alshabaab: A threat to East Africa... Christian and Muslim Militias Clash in Central Africa republic...*"

Amani twisted her new bangle then adjusted her rosary ring. "Am I a Christian, an African traditionalist or half African traditionalist- half Christian?"

She sneezed suddenly, waking her grandmother.

"I'm sorry, my granddaughter. It'll soon be over."

Mrs. Salo drove the vehicle into her expansive compound. She waved at the security guard and he saluted back.

"Mum, when I grow up I would like to be a security guard."

"Shut up, Junior. You have no idea what you are talking about," she said while driving to the garage.

Amani scratched her head as she read WhatsApp status updates on her android phone. Most of them were viral memes that Nchians were fond of forwarding to each other. She posted a text status: *"We are mourning the death of creativity in Nchi. Style up, dear friends."*

Her mother and grandmother sat on separate couches, waiting for the news. Junior was playing with his toy car. Melvin, their new houseboy, wiped the tables. He was younger than his predecessor but more talkative and full of laughter. As 9:00pm drew closer, Amani's mother waved at him to stop his chores. News was vital on that historical day.

"Top on our news stories tonight, Kingsley Pinto is the new president of Nchi republic… Elections violence marred South Feriani, Riverhood and Mani constituencies. In Riverhood constituency, an irate gang stomped into the polling station, roughed up the returning officer and left him bruised. It has not been established what led to the attack. In South Feriani and Mani constituencies, anti-riot officers were forced to use rubber bullets to disperse a rowdy defiant crowd protesting over what they described as 'an attempt to doctor elections results.' Nevertheless, no case of violence has been reported in the other three hundred constituencies of Nchi republic."

"God is great. Kingsley Pinto is our new president. Indeed we Hazundas are the chosen tribe," rejoiced Mrs. Salo.

Amani's grandmother giggled and said, "What if it were a Mbayuyu who had won the election, would there be any difference?"

"Stop talking like that, mama. Those braggarts are naturally dictators. They would lead us with an iron fist. That's why they will never rule Nchi," replied Mrs. Salo.

Amani remained silent. She signed into her Facebook account. An Australian international news agency had already updated its status: "*Africa plunges into violence.*" There were more than four thousand comments below the headline. Amani added her comment: "*Africa is not a village. It is the second largest continent on earth.*" Seconds later, another angry African posted his comment just below Amani's: "*Only three out of three hundred and three constituencies of Nchi were hit by mild violence that has been contained. Must stories from African nations be narrated in an exaggerated tone of poverty and violence?*"

Amani reverted her eyes to the television screen. President Kingsley Pinto was reading his acceptance speech. Kingsley proved to be a typical model of a boring speaker: standing still like a sculpture; eyes, unblinking; voice, monotonous and unnatural.

The head-of-state regurgitated barren cliché anthems of his predecessors: "My government will enhance equitable distribution of resources and opportunities in all regions of Nchi; eradicate tribalism, corruption and poverty."

He concluded his speech by reading a list of newly-appointed cabinet ministers and permanent secretaries. Thirty five out of forty ministries were headed by members of the president's ethnic group. The rest were occupied by tribe mates of the vice president.

"All contemporary African politicians have the same genetic structure," snapped Amani as she turned her attention back to Facebook. She clicked on the newly-elected president's page. *"Thank you fellow Nchians for voting peacefully. It's your victory. God bless Nchi,"* read president Pinto's latest post. Nuru had replied to a comment. Amani searched for his response in the 'comments' segment.

"Guys, there is only one tribe in Nchi republic called Nchi. One love," read Radi's comment.

Nuru had replied with a comment copied from his blog:

"It is only in Nchi where tribe and tribalism are synonyms. Welcome aboard- this is the famous nation of tribe and tribalism. By the way, what is tribe and what is tribalism?

Again, it is only in Nchi where one can feel offended when asked about one's tribal identity but see no offence in branding people from other tribes annihilating titles. Is that being Nchian?

In Nchi, the political elites and scholars condemn tribe. Tribe, they say, has led to unequal and inequitable distribution of resources and opportunities in their beloved country. Tribe is evil, they write. Tribe breeds bloodshed, they argue. Nchi is made up of one tribe: Nchi; they conclude. Rebellious scholars disagree; Nchi is made up of two tribes, namely: owners of the nation and children of the nation.

A keen observer, nevertheless; can't help but wonder, aren't the same political elites and scholars owners of the nation? Are they not the ones who spew disgusting phrases such as: 'So and so are targeting our tribe? Our vice chancellor is promoting lecturers from the wrong tribe? Members of tribe X should be kicked out of our ancestral land?'

Hallo, Nchians: Between tribe and tribalism, which one is evil?"

Amani reacted with love to his reply.

A new message from Derrick to Shiner's Organization WhatsApp group popped on her phone's screen. *"Hey buddies, I'm making early bookings for next week's International Peace Forum AGM. I shall be Africa's spokesperson. I promise to speak about our malnourished bodies, tree huts, pet crocodiles and flying brooms."*

C H A P T E R

19

Taifa University was unusually tranquil. Most students were still at home on long holiday. Members of International Peace Forum- Youth Category all over the world had converged in the university for their Annual General Meeting. That was the first meeting ever to be held in Africa since the inauguration of the peace group. Students were split into small groups of ten members.

Nuru's group was made up of a Jamaican, a Kenyan, an Afghan, a Nigerian, two Americans, a Tanzanian, a Nchian, a Canadian and a Chinese. By virtue of being Nchian, the host country, Nuru assumed the chairperson's position.

"Hallo, friends. My name is Nuru. I suggest we do the introductions first before we discuss anything."

"I think that sounds very boring. I beg we introduce ourselves as we socialize. For that reason, my name is Blessing Ajoke. Ajoke is spelt like a joke but don't dare call me a joke o. I'm from Nigeria."

"My name is Kipruto Chirchir from Kenya. I second her idea. You said your name is Ajoki?" he asked with a falling intonation making it sound like a statement, a common characteristic of Kenyan English.

"You are wrong, Kipruto. She said her name is Eijokee not Ajoki, I'm Bill from the US."

"The two of you are mutilating my name now. I said Ajoke not Ajoki or Eijokee."

"We've not heard the voices of our six silent friends. Tell us something about your country," said Nuru.

"My name is Cheryl Chambers. I'm from Jamaica, the sweet island of fish, bananas, coconuts and music. I feel good to be in Africa, the land of my ancestors."

"Which part of Africa is Jamaica?" The second American cut Cheryl short.

Everybody laughed at her ignorance.

"Hey girl! Jamaica is one of the Caribbean Islands," Cheryl barked.

"My name is Jean de Aime. I'm Canadian. I suggest we take a walk around this place and photograph hidden lions.'"

"I'm Marwa from Tanzania. Wild animals are not everywhere, Jean. They are only found in game reserves, game parks and national parks," he said, replacing "l" sounds with "r".

"By the way, I forgot to tell you something about my country, Nchi, at the beginning. It's one of the fastest growing economies in Africa but we've many challenges facing us. Corruption, tribalism and rampant unemployment are part of Nchi. We are not like Americans who can access national resources equally."

"I'm Lindsey Tracy, an American. It's kinda hilarious to say America is perfect. We've got challenges too."

"I agree with you, Lindsey. The US is not perfect, but our imperfections can't be compared to third world flaws."

"Come on, Bill. Imperfection is imperfection, whether from the first world or the third. Tell me America's racism is a lesser evil than Nchi's tribalism and I'll faint."

"Racism in America? You are nuts Lindsey."

"I'm not crazy but you are blind to the countless extra-judicial shootings of Blacks. Blind to the fact that White cops caught on camera shooting unarmed Blacks are free like air. Blind to the fact that it's acceptable to call Black Americans African-Americans, but an abomination to call White Americans European-Americans."

Bill shook his head and said, "Assuming that your imagined racism in America is real, can it be compared to Ebola in Africa or rampant gang rapes in India?"

"Bill, that's gospel according to the BBC and CNN. I wish they would have also informed you that Lagos is producing more new US dollar millionaires than Los Angeles and New York city," said Ajoke.

"Hi. I'm Lau Liang from China. I don't think foreign media houses are entirely responsible for portraying Africa as a hopeless continent. Africans too are to blame. I have read blogs by Africans, watched Nollywood movies, and one thing comes out; many Africans are apologetic of being Africans."

"I'm proudly African," interrupted Ajoke.

"No, you aren't. That blonde wig on your head is betraying you," belted Lau.

Ajoke snarled. Lau laughed at her.

Nuru chipped in, "I like the way this conversation is developing. Almost everyone is participating."

"That's right, Nuru, but we haven't heard the voice of this lady. Why are you silent?" Asked Lindsey while pointing at a young woman in a hijab.

"Hello. My name is Khadijah Abdi. I was born in Afghanistan, raised in Qatar and now attending university in England. I'm a Muslim and my religion puts emphasis on humility. Islam also advocates for total submission to Allah. Unfortunately, many Americans are intolerant of us. Why do you call us terrorists?"

"I politely disagree with you, Khadija. Americans are not intolerant of Muslims. We don't view you as terrorists. There are many Americans who are Muslims. Apart from that, the media spins many exaggerated news stories. For your information, there are many students studying Arabic language and Kiswahili language, an Arabic-African language, in several American Universities," said Bill.

"Point of correction, my brother. Kiswahili is a typical African language categorized under Bantu languages. It has more than ten dialects across East and Central Africa. The fact that Kiswahili has borrowed a few words from Arabic doesn't make it half Arabic. Need I say that English too has loaned some Kiswahili words like 'safari.' Does that make the English language half- Germanic half- Bantu?" Said Kipruto.

"I don't like the broken Kiswahili spoken by Kenyans. You keep on code switching from Kiswahili to English and other local languages," complained the Tanzanian.

"That's a type of slang called Sheng, spoken by a section of the urban Kenyan population."

"Good to learn about Kiswahili. Could the two of you teach us a few traditional Swahili songs?" requested Bill.

Marwa and Kipruto stared at each other blankly.

"Are those the preliminaries?" asked the Chinese as he took photos of them.

"Black people have music in their genes," commented Bill.

"Why are you people obsessed with skin colours? For your information, the majority of Africans have varying shades of chocolate complexion. Besides, haven't we introduced ourselves? Why can't you call us by our names? Or must you shout to the world about our differences?" lamented Ajoke.

"I'm sorry. I didn't intend to offend your race," apologized Bill.

Marwa started singing a popular Bongo hip hop song.

"That's hip-hop. We asked you to sing an ancient African song," said Bill.

"Why can't you Americans sing for us one ancient North American song?" howled Ajoke.

Bill became dumbfounded.

"Ok, let's forget about that. We're here to strengthen the global bonds. I'd like to see Lee fly back to China with Ajoke from Nigeria."

"Chai! You want me to starve to death o? How can I learn to start feeding on snakes, snails and dogs?"

"Have you forgotten why we are here? To demystify myths and appreciate our diversity," scowled the Chinese, slightly offended by Ajoke's joke.

"Once again I welcome you all to Nchi republic. Feel at home away from home. The program manager has informed me that you've just had a short interactive session in groups of ten. I hope it has been beneficial. As we prepare to usher in another activity, I'd like to get your reactions about the session. What have you learnt?" said Mohammed, the president of International Peace Forum- Nchi Chapter.

There were hands in the air.

"My name is Liz from Australia. I've always thought that Africa is only occupied by forests and primitive people. Today I've seen skyscrapers, good roads and modern technology in Africa. I'm enlightened."

"I'm Zambian. I used to think that all Americans are ignorant. Today I've met one who knows the history and geography of Zambia more than I do."

"I'm South African. I've interacted with a Brazilian and realized that Brazil and South Africa have a lot in common," she had a strong Xhosa accent that wowed the audience.

"My name is Kumar Patel. I'm from New Delhi India. I used to think that Japanese and Korean are different names referring to the same language. Now I can note the difference between the two languages."

"My name is Sarah Holland from the Netherlands. I've fallen in love with Africa. Africa has a good climate, beautiful landscape and hospitable people. I love Africa."

"As a Briton, I would be having zero knowledge about Africa but I refused to be ignorant. I read books by African writers telling their stories. Books helped me to explore the real Africa. Yes, I'm not a stranger in Nchi."

"Thank you. East Africans have a proverb that says, a good day is seen in the morning. I've no doubt today is going to be a wonderful day. Ladies and gentlemen, I hereby hand over the program to the program manager, Mr. Gray Abrahams," said Mohammed while shaking Gray's hand,

"Good morning, everybody. It's inspirational to see young intellects representing all the continents of the world coming together for the sake of global peace and unity. It's also amazing to appreciate the fact that this is a historical day. For the first time, the International Peace Forum –Youth Category is holding its annual conference in Africa. Apart from that, we've been joined by new members representing Somalia, Syria and Afghanistan. On behalf of the International Peace forum-Youth Category, I congratulate them and warmly welcome them to our network. Without much ado, I'll get to the climax of the event; awarding the champions of International Peace Forum-Youth Category. It has been a rigorous process to identify the heroes considering the fact that more members of this network are doing commendable jobs in making the planet earth a better place to live by fostering peace and unity in their respective societies. We are all heroes, but there are individuals among us who have done extraordinary deeds for the sake of peace and unity. Now, ladies and gentlemen, put your hands together for the world's youthful peace champions; members of Shiners Organization."

All the ten members of Shiners walked to the platform as the audience clapped.

"Under the leadership of Nuru Ntendo, members of Shiners Organization have been preaching peace. Nuru Ntendo and Amani Salo, both Literature students, have been posting poems that promote peace in Shiners Organization blog. Meanwhile, Derrick Mandela, a Computer Science major has developed a computer software program that uses microchips to detect fake ballot papers, unregistered voters and voters who have double registered. The system has tiny red bulbs, alarms and miniature cameras. Once a voter commits one of the crimes that I've mentioned, this is what will happen."

Mr. Gray Abrahams tried to insert two ballot papers into the ballot box. Sirens screamed and red lights twinkled on the platform.

"The system picks out the culprit's finger prints, uses them to decode all his/her biometric information from the registrar of persons' database, then sends the bio data via e-mail to the central police station. For non-citizens like me attempting to vote, this is what will be sent to the central police station."

Mr. Abrahams projected the message on the wall. A 3D photograph of Mr. Abrahams and his fingerprints were displayed on the wall. Below them were bold red letters that read; *Australian criminal-Gray Abrahams.*

"It has been established that post-elections violence in most parts of Africa is chiefly caused by electoral irregularities. I have no doubt that this innovation is invaluable in maintaining peace in Africa. Therefore, it is my honour to request the vice president of Nchi to present the following golden trophies and certificates of merit to members of Shiners Organization."

The vice president of Nchi stepped forward, accompanied by flickering camera lights.

"My sons and daughters, I'm pleased by your work. You've placed our country on the global map, I promise you that upon graduation, all of you are assured of securing jobs to serve in various capacities in the offices of Nchi National Unity and Cohesion. Your allowances and salaries will be fully catered for by the government. Congratulations once again," he whispered to them as he shook their hands.

Mr. Abrahams continued speaking, "There is a second category of award that shall be presented to members of International Peace Forum- Youth Category who have used their exceptional talents, skills and professional knowledge to foster peace and unity in their respective societies. In this category, the winners are: Irwin Yam from America for painting anti-racism cartoons; Shagari Hankali from Nigeria for writing and singing songs that preach harmony between Christians and Muslims in northern Nigeria; Nuru Ntendo and Amani Salo from Nchi for posting peace poems in Shiners Organization blog, and lastly; Derrick Mandela of Nchi for the groundbreaking innovation in ICT. Fellow citizens of the world, join me in congratulating our heroes by giving them a thunderous clap."

As the roar of the claps subsided, Mr. Abrahams said, "Each of the winner will receive one hundred thousand US dollars. On top of that, they'll be awarded a scholarship by the International Peace Forum to pursue a master's degree in their respective area of merit in one of the Ivy League Universities, six months after their graduation.

"It's also a great pleasure, ladies and gentleman, for me to state that the Senate of International Peace Forum -Youth Category nominated one of the young people standing in front of you to be the World Youth Peace Ambassador. Guess who it is? Well, the World Youth Peace Ambassador is Nuru Ntendo."

He was given a standing ovation amid screams and whistles.

"Your acceptance speech?"

"Your speech, please."

"Was he born and bred in Africa?"

"An African has been nominated?"

Nuru could hear part of the audience wondering aloud. A microphone was brought closer to him. He tried to compose himself but his emotions betrayed him. He broke into tears then recited the last stanza of his poem:

"Identity I Need to Know

Who am I?

Why is the world branding me names?

The poverty stricken?

The second citizen?

The struggling economist?

The sleeping giant?

The beggar?

The overgrown child?

Who am I?

I need to know my identity."

CHAPTER 20

$\mathcal{N}$uru studied his mother's figure of vigour on the gold framed portrait atop his desk. A photograph is worth a million words, so they say. To Nuru, a photograph was worth a million features. Each day, his mother's portrait bore a new feature: horrifying dark scar on the neck, evil eyes or sneering lips. That day, a novel bond had been formed between Nuru and his mother's photograph. A strong wave of good energy seemed to be flowing to him from his mother's portrait.

The horrible dark scar had vanished mysteriously. Her sneering lips formed a gentle curve on the photograph; a smile. Mrs. Ntendo's eyes were brighter than ever and full of life. Nuru smiled back at the photograph. The wall clock ticked more loudly.

"How time flies," he sighed.

Exactly two and a half years ago, he was crowned the world's peace ambassador for his efforts in fighting tribalism, a vice that's yet to be snuffed out of Nchi republic. In only two months, he would be flying out of Nchi to the United States of America alongside Amani and Derrick.

The main door to his office was opened, revealing his secretary.

"Good morning, sir. There is a mister Craig at the reception who'd like to seek your assistance in reconciling with his family."

"What's his second name?"

"I'm sorry, sir. I was unable to capture it due to the rapidity of his speech, but it was something like Sola."

"It is our constitutional obligation to unite and reconcile families, friends and tribes split by the past ethnic clashes that have been witnessed in Nchi. Allow him to get into my office and I shall be glad to be of service to him."

Three minutes later, somebody rapped on the door of the office.

"Come in please," said Nuru.

A middle -aged man walked to his desk. His face looked friendly and familiar to Nuru but he could not recall where he had met the man.

"Welcome, sir. Have a seat please."

"Thank you," said the man as he occupied a seat adjacent to Nuru.

"My name is Nuru Ntendo, the coordinator of Nchi National Unity and Cohesion, Goba chapter. And you, Sir?"

"I'm Craig Salo. Thank you for the good job you are doing."

"By the way, you look familiar. Have we ever met?" Asked Nuru.

"I doubt if we've ever met before. If we met then you were barely two years old. I left this country twenty two years ago for Italy with my ex-lover."

'*The world is a cycle,*' Nuru's ring tone interrupted them.

"Excuse me….Hallo, dad."

"How are you doing, son? I've good news for you," said Mr. Ntendo.

"What is it, dad? Has Professor Pius been arrested?" Inquired Nuru.

"No. The letter that your mum wrote to the ministry of internal affairs has borne some fruits. The government will grant each victim of Bande tribal violence 50,000 Nchi pounds," he replied.

"That's very little."

"Stop being ungrateful like your mother. She almost got arrested for telling off a senior employee at the ministry of internal affairs."

"Dad, perpetrators of Bande tribal violence are at large; laughing at us. As if that is not enough, Professor Pius is the minister of defense. Isn't this a joke to justice?"

"Listen, son. A journey of a thousand miles starts with a single stride. This could be the beginning of better things. We shall talk later. Your mum and I are heading towards your office right now. We have a document from the minister of internal affairs that requires your signature."

"You are welcome."

Nuru turned to his guest and said, "Sorry for the interruption. You said you left Nchi twenty two years ago?"

"That's true, Nuru. I met a White woman in a tourism agency that I used to work as a clerk, and it was lust at first sight from both parties. We spent nights in hotel rooms and clubs and partied endlessly. The closer I became to her, the more I forgot about my young family of one infant daughter and wife. I flew with Veronique to France- her native country. I had no travel documents but nobody questioned me. Veronique is a powerful woman who knows big people. France did not recognize me. I became an illegal immigrant. Playing hide and seek with cops became part of my lifestyle."

"What was the profession of your lover?"

"I'm ashamed; she was a drug baron. I also used to traffic drugs. Veronique had a network of drug cartels in many countries here in Africa, Europe, Asia, the Caribbean Islands and Latin America. In our country, the majority of the drug cartels are high profile politicians. I think that's why I flew out of this country with Veronique without being asked for travel documents."

"I can't believe."

"It's incredible but what I'm about to tell you is more unbelievable and it is in line with some of our so called politicians. They are devil incarnates, that's the only euphemism I can use to describe them. Many intelligent students and industrious Nchians have witnessed their lives take a nose dive courtesy of malicious politicians."

"How does that happen?" Wondered Nuru.

"During campaign periods, politicians seek fame through various ways. They'll go to an extent of promising to give scholarships to bright and needy students to study abroad. Indeed they'll award the students the scholarships, but after getting what they want, that is power, they often withdraw funds. Many such students end up being bankrupt abroad and drop out of college. I've seen thousands of them seek refuge in commercial sex, robbery with violence and drug trafficking. Some of them even found a haven in our network and we would hire them to peddle illicit drugs."

"You didn't have a conscience?"

"Illegal drugs were controlling me rather than brains. I later learnt that I unconsciously had my first encounter with cocaine in a hotel room that I used to share with Veronique. From then, I became an addict and couldn't do without them. Drugs are destructive, my son. I developed multiple medical complications and had a series of memory lapse. I thank God, I'm alive. Two of my work mates passed away due to drugs and substance abuse."

"What about your family? Haven't you been in touch with them?" Asked Nuru.

"I lost contact with the outside world completely from the day I left Nchi for France. If I hadn't met Joshua, a France based Nchian evangelist, in an underground train, I wouldn't be here. I give all glory to God. He converted me and led me to the embassy of Nchi."

"Officials at the embassy took care of your flight back home?"

"Absolutely. I was also given the address to your office. I was informed that your main responsibility is to re-unite families that split up many years ago," said Mr. Salo.

"We re-unite families that were separated physically and emotionally by the past tribal clashes. We've access to the data base of the registrar of persons."

"I'm not a victim of tribal violence. Can you help me meet my wife and daughter called Amani Salo?"

"You mean Amani Salo is your daughter!" Exclaimed Nuru.

"Yes, she is. Do you know her?"

"Just a minute please."

Nuru took his handset and called her.

"Good morning, Amani. There is a guest in my office who would like to meet you. It's very urgent. Please just leave your office and come to my office with your mum."

"Who is he or she?" Asked Amani.

"A very important person."

"Ok. We'll be there in less than ten minutes. After all, Tibo and Goba are five kilometers apart."

Nuru ended the call and shifted his attention to Mr. Salo.

"Yes, sir. I know your daughter. She is on her way to my office."

"Thank you, son."

There was another rap on the door.

"Get in, the door is open."

Nuru's parents walked into his office.

"Welcome, dad and mum. Have a pleasure to meet Mr. Craig Salo. Mr. Craig, meet my parents, Mr. and Mrs. Ntendo."

After the introductions, the three men and woman embarked on a hot political debate. Mrs. Ntendo threw the first kick by criticizing Nchi men for being scared of a woman president. Mr. Salo defended Nchi men by arguing that God created man to be the head of the family. Nuru and his father cheered him.

The office door was still ajar. Amani pushed it and entered accompanied by her mother, grandmother and Junior. Mrs. Salo's eyes landed on Mr. Salo. She did not believe her eyes.

"Oh! My sweet lovely wife," Mr. Salo said as he outstretched his arms.

Mrs. Salo whimpered. Amani's grandmother placed her arms on her head and raised her eyebrows. Junior clutched his mother's leg.

"Are you my father?" screamed Amani.

"Is it Amani? I'm your biological dad."

"Oh daddy!" Exclaimed Amani as she jumped up and hugged him.

"Get away from that beast," said Mrs. Salo.

"Mummy, he's my dad."

"I'm sorry, my wife."

"You are sorry?"

"Why did you disown my daughter?" Yelled Amani's grandmother.

"Mummy, granny. Please give my dad time to express himself."

"Yes," agreed Mr. Ntendo.

There was silence in the office. Mr. Salo cleared his throat and narrated his encounter with the French woman at the tourism agency to his departure from France. He produced documents and photographs to back up his story. There was a long silence after his narration.

"My wife, my mother-in law, my daughter," he took a short pause when his eyes landed on Junior. Junior covered his face out of fear, "I wronged you. I betrayed you. I'm here begging your pardon. I've learnt my lesson the hard way. Kindly, I beseech you, accept me back."

"My son-in –law, you are welcome back," said Amani's grandmother.

"Isn't it too late?"

"Trust me, my dear wife. With true love, it's never too late," replied Mr. Salo.

He embraced her.

"Mummy. Is he God? Is he God my father? He has visited us?" Screamed Junior.

"Many years after your departure from Nchi, I met another man who impregnated me and disappeared into the thin air. The result of our relationship was this young boy called Junior," said Amani's mother in Hazunda language to hide her message from Junior.

"I still love you, my wife. It's understandable. Come here, my son."

He held Junior in the air.

"Junior, I'm not God but I'm your father. My name is Craig Salo."

"I love you my husband," uttered Mrs. Salo.

"Thank you, Nuru. Thank you very much, my love," said Amani.

"Is he the Buba young man you've been telling me about?" Mrs. Salo inquired, visibly irritated.

"Yes, I'm her boyfriend and I love her," replied Nuru.

"You are still in love with this Hazunda woman?" cried Mrs. Ntendo.

"Don't embarrass me, mum. Have you forgotten my position in the world? Besides, Amani and I will be flying out of the country to study Literature courtesy of our tireless efforts to fight tribalism. Why are you letting us down? Please don't. We're living in a new world of love."

Amani's grandmother used that moment to talk about her daughter's dream that occurred two and a half years ago.

"In this world, experience has taught me that there are three categories of lovers. I will talk about them in ascending order. In category one, we have forced lovers-people who were forced to be together by either their relatives or friends. In category two, we have cosmetic lovers- people who force themselves to be together and pretend that they are truly in love, in this case they want to maintain class purity or one party is materialistic; last but the best, we've got soulmates who were destined to be together. Lovers who were born for each other," said Mr. Salo.

"And nothing can tear them apart," added Amani's grandmother.

"And that's why our parents have been brought together in my office mysteriously."

"My people, I hereby beg you to bless my relationship with Nuru. Kindly grant us the power to start courting officially," requested Amani.

Mrs. Ntendo broke into a famous Buba pre-wedding song. Everyone joined her in the singing and dancing except Mrs. Salo.

"Hallo!" interjected Nuru, "This is a very auspicious day and I suggest we finalize it in Africanah Hotel where engagement rings shall be exchanged. We'll purchase them on our way."

"Yes," agreed Amani's grandmother before singing another Buba pre-wedding song.

Mrs. Ntendo laughed at her accent. She then turned to Mrs. Salo and said, "Mama Amani, give it a try. I won't make fun of your accent."

"Rubbish! My daughter will never get married to your Buba son. I hate you people," said Mrs. Salo at the top of her voice.

"No!" Cried Amani.

Nuru placed his right arm on her shoulders and said, "You're mine forever."

"Yes, she is yours forever. I bless your union," said Amani's grandmother.

Mrs. Salo attempted to grab Nuru by the collar but her mother blocked her with a walking stick. Mr. Salo and the Ntendos formed a human shield around Nuru and Amani.

"Buba man, I will ensure that it ends in tears," she said before storming out of the office.

When Mrs. Salo's footsteps became inaudible, Amani's grandmother said, "Your blessed relationship will endure all storms. Now let's go to Africanah Hotel."

She led the way. In Buba culture, an elderly woman's opinion on marital issues was final. It was believed that any form of rebellion would attract tragedy. Mrs. Salo's actions had made the Ntendos to develop pessimism towards Nuru and Amani's relationship. However, they followed Amani's grandmother to the parking lot, scared of facing their ancestors' wrath.

Outside, the sunny sky had been replaced by rain bearing clouds. In the next few minutes, a heavy rain would fall.

Nuru walked to his car and opened all the doors.

"Welcome on board," he said.

Mrs. Ntendo helped Amani's grandmother to get into the car. Amani sat at the co-driver's seat. When everybody settled, Nuru urged them to fasten their seat belts. He started the engine and drove off towards Africanah Hotel.

Above Nuru's head- just below the rear view mirror- was a dangling globe with the words, *"I am because you are. You are because we are. We are because you are."* The colour of the words changed in accordance with the angle at which one viewed them.

#END

www.ingramcontent.com/pod-product-compliance
Lightning Source LLC
Chambersburg PA
CBHW030749110726
47900CB00008B/2519